Son of an Earl...
Sold for a Slave

Son of an Earl...
Sold for a Slave

By David B. Weems
Illustrated by Mauro Magellan

A FIREBIRD PRESS BOOK

PELICAN PUBLISHING COMPANY
Gretna 1998

Library of Congress Cataloging-in-Publication Data

Weems, David B.
Son of an earl—sold for a slave / by David B. Weems ;
illustrated by Mauro Magellan.
p.   cm.
Summary: After being kidnapped and sold as a bond servant in
colonial America, fifteen-year-old James, the son of a Scottish
earl, struggles with his identity and his loyalty to the
Revolutionary cause.
ISBN 1-56554-562-1
1. United States—History—Revolution, 1775–1783—Juvenile
fiction. [1. United States—History—Revolution, 1775–1783-
-Fiction.] I. Magellan, Mauro, ill. II. Title.
PZ7.W42244So 1992
[Fic]—dc20   92-27917
                                                       CIP
                                                        AC

*The word "Pelican" and the depiction of a pelican are
trademarks of Pelican Publishing Company, Inc., and are
registered in the U.S. Patent and Trademark Office.*

Manufactured in the United States of America
Published by Pelican Publishing Company, Inc.
1000 Burmaster Street, Gretna, Louisiana 70053

To Charys.

Contents

Son of an Earl...
Sold for a Slave

Chapter One

Something Lost

I STARED AT THE BARE PLACE on the rock wall. There was a gap in the line of three paintings that stood on the floor. Three. I had left four there.

I went to the wooden door and pulled it open to let in some light. It did no good. One of the paintings was gone.

There is a story in the Bible about a bad storm in the time of King Ahab. The only warning they had before the storm was a tiny cloud. It was no bigger than a man's hand, according to the Scripture. The empty place there on the wall was such a sign. I could not even dream of the things it would cause—things that would come back to prey on me again and again over many years and across an ocean. If I had seen what was to come, I would have gone straight to my father and told all. My life would have been a different story.

As it was, I saw only that Father would be angry about the money that he paid the French artist. If I kept the loss a secret, I might find it before he noticed. So, instead of calling for help, I went on with what I had come to do. I got out some of the paints that the Frenchman had left there and began to dab at one of the paintings.

"James," a voice called.

I went to the door and looked out. Elizabeth frowned into the damp wind that tangled her long, black hair.

"James," she called again, looking out at the cliff.

11

"Here. In the loft above the stable," I yelled.

She came into the stable and stopped at the foot of the stairway. She put the last piece of a scone into her mouth and licked her fingers before she spoke.

"We've been looking for you. What are you doing here?"

"Painting."

"Painting? Why?"

"I'm going to be an artist."

"What an odd idea. Two years ago, you wanted to be a soldier."

"Yes, for Prince Charlie."

"First soldier, now artist," she said, coming up the stairs. "What will it be next?"

"Soldier again, if Charlie returns, but I wonder if we shall ever see him in Scotland again."

"Well, you have grown up a little. But an artist? Really, James. Does your father know?"

"No, but Aunt Alice does."

"Of course, she would know. We'd better go. Your father is angry."

"What about?" I asked, wondering if he knew about the lost painting.

"Your birthday dinner. People are hungry."

"Oh I forgot," I said, putting away the paints. Then I thought I knew who had been in the loft. "Did you take the Frenchman's painting?"

"The one of you in the tartan? Of course not. Where was it?"

"Right here. I saw it yesterday."

"That can put you in a fine fix."

"Yes, Father won't like it."

"That's not what I meant. What about the ban on tartans? Has your father seen it?"

"Not yet."

"I thought so. He wouldn't—"

"My father is a true Scot."

"True enough to break English law?"

"It's a stupid law. Why should the English have the right to tell us what to do?"

"Because they won. Isn't there a prison term?"

"There's supposed to be."

"How long?"

"Six months for the first offense."

"And for the second?"

"Shipment overseas."

"So, James, you just had to fly in the face of the law with that tartan. Didn't I tell you it was a silly thing to do? If you go to prison for six months..."

"It's an old law—over twenty-five years old—and times change. Besides, they would never hold me, the son of an earl."

"How do you know? If you think that I will marry anyone who..."

"As for that, our fathers agreed upon it."

"You think that I have no say? What are you doing now?"

"Taking a pair of my paintings to show at dinner."

"Now? When you are already late?"

"I can't wait to see how they like these," I said.

When we got to the castle, Elizabeth stopped at the glass door of a cabinet to pat her hair into shape around the smooth skin of her oval face; then we went into the dining room. Some of the guests smiled when they saw us. Father frowned.

"It's about time," he said.

I set up the paintings on the sideboard. A few people came over to see them. Father turned to look and froze.

"What's this?" he asked.

"This," I said, waving a hand at them, "is my future."

People stopped talking. Aunt Alice, who had lived with us since Mother died, came over to where we stood.

"Don't you love his paintings? That one of Robert the Bruce in the cave with the spider is nice, but I think this one of young Flora MacDonald helping Prince Charlie into the boat is lovely."

"A strong woman," someone said.

"Yes. The English would have caught Charlie if she hadn't been there to help him escape," said another.

"James," Father said, bending over the Bruce painting. "If you want to be an artist, you must sharpen your eye."

"I copied the cave from the one in the cliff under the castle," I said.

"But the spider should have eight legs, James."

I said nothing. My fifteenth birthday had gone sour—first the lost painting, then this.

"I don't know a lot about art, but I do know that the first rule in any work is to get your facts right," Father said. "And speaking of art, did Monsieur Genet finish that portrait of you? Where is it?"

"Yes," said Elizabeth. "And James posed for it wearing—"

"It is almost done," I said, frowning at Elizabeth to stop her. "Do we have to have it now?"

"Let's eat. We can see it later," said Uncle Mark, showing a toothy smile. He was much younger than Father. In the uprising, he sided with the English, who made him an officer. Father was in Italy at the time, so the English never knew that his heart was with Charlie. That is why he was allowed to keep his lands and his title as the earl of Gour.

"Look at this," I said to Elizabeth to get her away from talk of the lost painting. "This boat is the one we used on your father's lake." Her father, the laird of MacTay, owned almost as much land as my father.

"I plan to give this to Flora MacDonald someday," I said.

"Do you think it is good enough? The people seem flat."

"Do you mean that you don't like it?"

"Flora is a middle-aged woman now. She must have enough paintings by real artists."

"She doesn't have this one. It may be the only one like it in the whole world. The idea behind it—"

"Ideas! You sound like a Frenchman. It's the real things that count."

"Don't give the French credit for everything," said Thomas

Lindsay, my tutor from Kirkaldy. "Just yesterday, I heard someone say that Rousseau was the first to deny the right of kings to mistreat people. A Scot named John Mair taught that notion to John Knox two hundred and fifty years ago. He got it from the Bible. An idea like that can change the world."

"Who wants to change it?" Elizabeth asked. She turned to me again. "After we are married, you will leave art to the artists—painting is no work for a gentleman."

That stung me. "My paintings have a message," I said.

"What will be, will be. You can't change that."

"Well said, Elizabeth."

That opinion came from Reverend West, the Presbyterian parson from the village. His sermons always said that life was planned for us. People accepted that and, all in all, so did I. Life was good for an earl and the son of an earl.

The next morning I wasn't so sure.

Chapter Two

A Job for Me

WHEN A SERVANT WOKE ME the next morning, the first thing I thought of was the lost painting. One person came to mind who might have hidden it from me as a game. I went to the stable and dug into every bin and box. I had just gone through a chaff box when Duncan, our gardener, found me.

"The laird wants you in the library," he said.

Father was looking over some account books on the table.

"It's time for you to run the land for me," he said.

Me? The idea had never come into my head. Surely I could get someone to do it for me.

"We could get a tacksman," I said.

"Tacksmen are drones. Their days are over. You lose profit and you might get another Lynch."

"Lynch? The man with the scar on his neck?"

"Yes, the one who stole from us."

"That was a long time ago."

"Not so long. It has been just four years. Lynch is in prison now. Anyway, it's time for you to learn."

His eyes burned up at me from his dried-up face. I saw, for the first time, that he was an old man. "No more tacksmen," he said, "and no more letting crofters draw lots for their land. Give a man the same plot year after year, and he'll try to take care of it. This is 1773, not the Dark Ages."

He went on about his plans for the land—the use of lime

and manure, new crops, and such. I heard his words but I began to daydream. Then, all at once, I came back to hear him say, "Your uncle Mark can go with you on Monday. He knows the highlands and can show you where to get the rent money."

When he was done talking, I got my paints and went out on the cliff. I set up an easel and began to paint. It wasn't going right; then a fog came in from the sea. As the scene before me faded into the silver mist, I put down the brush and sat on a rock.

"Who stole your scone?"

It was Jennie Duncan, the daughter of our gardener. The way she knew my mood, even before I spoke, irked me.

"Go away," I said.

"Aren't we sour?"

"Isn't it time for you to help at the castle?"

"Way past time. That's why I'm here with you. What's this?"

She looked at the canvas I had quit painting and shook her head. That reminded me of something I wanted to ask her.

"Jennie, did you hide that painting?"

"What painting?"

"The one the Frenchman did of me."

"You? No. Who would want a painting of you?" She pushed her hair back from her eyes so she could watch my face with a quick side glance. This was a habit of hers.

"It's no joke, Jennie. I need it."

"Well, I don't have it." She pointed to the easel. "Why does that have three legs?"

"Three legs make it stand firm anywhere."

"Aye," she said, switching from proper English to a Scottish singsong. "And have ye no such spiders?"

I grabbed a brush, but she ran away before I could dab her freckled face with green paint. So, the story about the spider had gotten to all the servants. I kicked the easel, and it went over the edge of the cliff. Then I saw the board of paints lying on the ground. I picked it up and threw it as hard as I could. It sailed up and out, then down into the fog.

When I went into the castle, Elizabeth and her parents were leaving. She stopped and waited for me. As I neared, she made her face into a pout, a look that I always found so winning.

"I saw you out there. It ill suits you to be chummy with a housemaid."

"Jennie hasn't found her place in life yet."

"She will find it when I have a say."

Elizabeth went to the carriage; then she came back.

"You may kiss me goodbye, James. Don't muss my hair."

I kissed her and I thought, in three years or less we would be married. After that, I would be one of the richest men in Scotland.

On Monday morning, Duncan brought two horses from the stable. He tied them to a post and began to pull weeds from a flower bed. When Uncle Mark came out, I started to go to the horses.

"Wait," Uncle mark said to me. Then he called to Duncan. "Over here with those horses. Now! We are in a hurry."

Duncan got the horses without a word. Father and Aunt Alice came out to see us off, so we said farewell to them and rode away. I wore my new sporran, the money pouch that Father gave me on my birthday. As we rode along the old carriageway that led to the road, Jennie came out.

"Where are you going?" she asked.

"To the highlands."

"How long?"

"Maybe forever."

"Will ye no come back again?" she quoted from Scotland's most loved song—and the title I gave to my painting of Flora and Charlie. Jennie began to sing the song.

> *Will ye no come back again?*
> *Will ye no come back again?*
> *Bonnie Charlie, we can win,*
> *Will ye no come back again?*

"I've told you before, that third line isn't right," I said.

"I learned it from you."

"I know that. When I first sang it for you, I didn't know all the words, so I made up the 'we can win' part."

"It was fun anyway."

It was like a shared secret, I thought, but it no longer seemed right for me to share any kind of secret with a housemaid.

"I've got to go, Jennie."

"What will ye bring me?"

Her voice had a teasing tone, so I did not answer.

"Ye might find some bluebells. They be all gone here."

I rode on.

"Will ye no bring me at least a wee daisy?" she asked, pushing her hair back to look sideways at me.

"If I must bring you a flower, I'll look for a Stinking Willy," I said. That was what we called the plant the English called "Sweet William." They named it for the Duke of Cumberland, the man who butchered our Scots at Culloden.

I urged my pony into a trot to catch up with Uncle Mark. As we rode along the road, I looked back and saw her wave. A hill came between us and she was gone, but the scene was frozen in my mind. The old redrock castle with Jennie standing in the tree-lined path—one hand holding some flowers high in the air. That, I thought, would make a great painting. An odd feeling came over me then. Maybe it was because unless Father kept her on as a housemaid, Jennie would soon leave the servant hall to either work or marry. Housemaid was the lowest job for a poor lass. Later, she would move up to scullery maid, kitchen maid, and, at last, cook. Life was planned for me and it was planned for Jennie as well.

I looked back again, but all I saw was a hill. I had left the neat world of Gour Castle behind. It was good that I could not see what lay ahead of me.

Chapter Three

A Yellow Dog

As we rode into the hills, we passed shaggy brown cattle that stared back at us. A red deer crossed our path. At night, we stopped at a house where our host gave us food and beds. The next day broke with gusts of wind and flying clouds. By night, rain was falling. We found some mud-colored, thatch-covered huts. Smoke came out of a hole in each roof. We stopped at the first hut and went inside.

The smoke from the fire filled the room and made my eyes water. Children sat around us on the dirt floor, nearly naked. They were waiting for supper, a meal of cooked kale and oat cakes. The woman rolled out coarse oatmeal in beef fat, then baked the cakes on a black piece of iron over the low fire in the middle of the floor. Such food. At home, we had soups, veal cooked with herbs and mushrooms, vegetables from Duncan's garden, candied fruits, and high teas with rich scones or other breads. Why was there such a difference in food? Then I realized that these people would not know fine food if they had it.

As we waited for the oat cakes to cook, I stared at the people in the hut. To wear such rags, they must have no other clothing. Had they never heard of soap? As I looked at them, I felt sure that even water must be hard to get in the highlands.

We ate our oat cakes while the stick of wood that lit the hut burned low. At the last glow, the children lay down on the dirt floor to sleep. Their parents made room for us on some skins behind the wicker curtain that divided the one room. I lay awake, annoyed by the hard earth bed and the odors in the little hut. Sleep came at last, and I awoke at dawn to see that Uncle Mark was gone. I found him outside.

"Let's find a better place to stay next time," I said.

"There are no better places here."

"Then take another road. I don't like this place and I don't like these people. I don't want to stay with them again."

"You have to. They are our renters."

"Our renters? Why don't we get better renters?"

"Renters are renters, if they pay."

The man from the hut came out, and Uncle Mark asked him for the rent. The man, who walked with a limp, went to the hut and came back with a pound note. He promised the rest later.

"That won't do," Uncle Mark said, his face set.

"B-b-but I have to save s-s-some for s-s-seed."

"Rent comes first. Pay now or get out."

The man stepped back. He hobbled into the hut and came out with another pound note.

"It will be three pounds next year," Uncle Mark said.

"D-d-don't know how we can p-p-pay that much."

"Work harder."

Later, after we had gone, he said, "You must be firm with these people or you get nothing from them."

"What happens if they don't have the money?" I asked.

"We'll drive them off and put sheep on the land. That's what some owners are doing."

"How did we get this land that is so far from home?"

"The first earl won it in battle."

And I, as the ninth earl, would inherit it from my father. The rents we got at each hut would be mine. Maybe, after all, I could tolerate such people once a year.

When we were done with that lot of huts, we had fourteen

pounds in all. The rest of the tour was very similar to the beginning. We stopped at dirty hovels, ate stale food, and haggled over rents. One day, Uncle Mark said we were done.

"Take the money to the Bank of Scotland in Edinburgh. I'm going back to Fife."

"How far is it to Edinburgh?" I asked.

"Less than a day's ride. I'll show you."

He drew a map in the dirt.

"About three hours south of here you will reach a stream. Cross it and take the left fork of the road. After you go over a hill, you will find an inn. You can get a good meal there."

He drew another line, showing me how to find the ferry that crossed the Firth to Edinburgh; then he rode away.

I found the inn some time after noon. It was almost empty. I sat down and ordered a plate of vegetables and pickled pork, topped off with a pudding and a pot of tea. A man with a dark beard and long hair tucked into his collar came in. He looked around, saw me, then came toward my table. I looked away.

"Be ye James Gour?"

I put down my cup and faced him.

"I have a message for ye."

How could he? How did he know me?

"It's the old laird."

"My father?"

"Aye. Went sick Wednesday. In Edinbory now. A lady asks ye to meet her there."

That would be Aunt Alice. Edinburgh had good doctors, but would Father leave the castle? Maybe he was too sick to care.

"Where in Edinburgh?"

"A small inn. I can take ye. A shilling would make it right."

I reached into my sporran and tossed a shilling onto the table.

"There's your shilling. Get me to my aunt before night and you shall have another."

"'Tis a bonny sporran there," he said.

"It was a birthday gift from my father."

"Aye. It's three of the clock. Best we go."

He had no horse, so he climbed on behind me. Before we had been gone a half hour, the horse threw a shoe.

"Bad luck," the man said.

We found a crofter who said he would look after the horse, then we continued on foot. It was dark when we took the ferry across the Firth. As we went down a dark street, a drum sounded ahead of us and someone called out, "Gardyloo." The man with me quickly stepped to the wall of a building, but I was hit by slops and garbage thrown from an upstairs window.

"Forgot to warn ye about gardyloo," the man said.

I tried to shake off as much of the stinking swill as I could. Some of it hit an old yellow dog that was lying on the steps of the building. He got up and walked away, looking back at me as if I had hit him. We went on, turned a few corners, and stopped at a building in a narrow street. The man rapped on a door. It opened and we went up on the step, but an old woman sniffed at me and shook her head.

"He can't come in here like that."

"We had a mishap," the man said.

"Don't care what ye had, he can't come in."

"Ye wouldna' put him oot if it wasna' his fault?"

"Aye, I would put him oot if he got in."

"He wants to see his aunt. How aboot some dry clothes?"

"Take him oot. Then we'll see aboot clothes."

"Wait here," the man said, going in.

As I stood on the step, I looked up and down the dark street. The building across the way was half down with a sagging roof and empty windows. Why had Aunt Alice come here? All of the city that I had seen was like this. I didn't like the old woman either. Should I leave? But no, the

man had spoken for me. He was my only link to Aunt Alice and Father.

The man brought some garments, and I put them on in an alley at the side. The new things seemed tight on me.

"Give me the shoes too. I'll get them cleaned for ye," the man said. I gave them to him and went to the candlelit doorway in my bare feet. A large, yellow dog that was lying on the step, got up when he saw me coming and walked stiffly away. I saw him but gave him no thought. I looked at my clothing. Instead of good woolens, I now wore old cotton rags.

"These things are dirty," I said.

"They will do ye until the morn."

"Where is Aunt Alice?"

"Upstairs."

We went up a narrow stairway and turned down a dark hall. The man opened the door.

"There's no light here," I said.

I turned to go for a candle, but he shoved me into the room and slammed the door. As I whirled around to push it open, I heard a bolt move. When I shook the door, it moved a little. There was a sound on the other side and the door became tighter. There was another noise and the door felt as solid as a rock wall. A faint light came from a window. I went to it but saw only the shape of some bars outside. I called out. Then I went back and beat on the door. I beat and yelled until I heard steps.

"Be quiet." It was the old woman.

"Do you think you can do this to the son of an earl? Do you know what will happen to you when my father finds out?"

"Go to sleep."

"I'm James Gour."

"No one can hear ye but me."

"I'll give you money."

I reached for my sporran, but it was gone. Of course. I

took it off in the alley. I could hear the old woman cackling, then she went away.

I sank onto the only thing in the room, a narrow cot. Why had it never entered my mind that I was in danger? Who could have imagined this? It made no sense.

Chapter Four

Something Found

I SAT ALONE IN THE LITTLE ROOM. What were they going to do with me? I lay on the cot and tried to sleep, but I tossed to and fro asking myself why. Why was I here? Why didn't I ask the man for proof that he came from Aunt Alice? Why did I trust him after I saw how he looked at my money pouch?

Oh, but he was sly to ask for money from me. If he had not done that, I might have seen his game. He must have planned the whole day.

"Bad luck," he had said when the horse lost a shoe. That was too much bad luck for one day: Father's illness, the shoe, gardyloo, and the old woman. All too much.

Wait, there was more—a dog—an old, yellow dog that walked as if each step hurt him. Such a dog was on the steps where someone threw slops on me. Another dog of the same kind was here. No. It was the same dog. We must have made a circle and come back again. The old woman was the one who poured the slops on me.

How did the man get us here at just the right time for gardyloo? If the man who gave the signal was one of the gang, it would be easy. That was it—a gang. Why hadn't I run from this seedy place when they left me alone on the steps? I would be ready if I got another chance.

Who would believe that they would try to rob James Gour? Father would get them back. When they tried to sell

31

my good clothing, it would be known. The money pouch had my initials cut into the leather. These thoughts made me feel better.

Why didn't the man just grab the pouch and run? That would have been easier. Again, why were they holding me? I felt a new twist of fear in my middle.

I spent the night going over the events of the day. Did I sleep? I dozed a bit, then I heard a sound at the door.

"Let's go."

The thump, thump of feet on the wood floor told me that there were two of them. Some hands grabbed each of my arms and pulled me down the stairs. We went out a back door at the first glow in the east. The ground behind the building was so steep that we slipped and slid down the slope until we came to a flat place. The bearded man left me with the other, a huge fellow, while he stirred a burned-out fire. I tried to talk to the big man.

"My father will pay you well if you get me out of here," I said.

He looked at me but said nothing. The bearded man must have heard my voice. He looked around and said, "Be quiet or we'll gag ye."

The fire blazed up and lit the ground around it. I saw part of a shoe and a leather strap in the flames—and on the strap was my money pouch. Another hour and all would be ashes, and so would my hopes for rescue. What were they going to do with me? I would recognize them anywhere. Fear hit me again.

We went down into a thick fog to the water. The men found a boat in some bushes and put me in it. That gave me hope of jumping out, but they tied my hands and feet. One of them got a three-cornered hat from the bottom of the boat and shoved it onto my head. It was dirty but felt good in the chilly fog.

The men rowed us to the far bank. We went ashore and walked eastward. As the fog lifted, I saw a sailing ship in the water. We went near some houses, off to our left, but I saw no one about.

The men took me to a stone building where we found some men standing in a line in a big room. A plump man in a good broadcloth suit sat at a table. From the talk, I learned that he was an Englishman, Captain Chase, of the ship *Minerva*. The sight of the captain gave me new hope. A clerk sat beside Chase, writing in a book. Some of the men who waited along the wall before me wore dirty rags and had bad teeth. They had a look of despair about them. Others were clean but poorly dressed. One by one, they went to the table and talked to the captain. Some of them signed papers. At last, it was my turn. I spoke first.

"I am James Gour, son of the earl of Gour."

Captain Chase looked at me, then at my dirty rags and bare feet. The bearded man laughed. At that, the captain laughed.

"My father will reward you—," I began.

"No doubt, with silver and gold," said the captain and laughed again. Then he looked at the bearded man. "Why is he here?"

"Caught with a tartan. Second time. Convicted for shipment."

"Papers?"

"We took a boat from Edinbory and he tried to get away. He turned over the boat and lost the papers."

"I can't take a prisoner without papers from a magistrate."

The bearded man jerked his head at the big man. The giant dragged me away and stood before me so I couldn't see the men at the table. I heard low voices, then the captain's voice, a bit louder.

"What's his name?"

"John Scott."

"James Gour," I yelled.

"Give us his hat," the bearded man said.

The big man took off my hat and handed it to the other who turned it inside out. There, under the top, was the name, "J. Scott."

"And we have a witness," he said.

He went out and came back with a scrawny fellow who gave his name as Cane. He had a package with him.

"Have you ever seen this lad?" the captain asked, pointing at me.

"Aye."

"When and where?"

"A twelvemonth ago. He worked for the old laird at Gour."

"What's his name?"

"John Scott."

"A lie," I said. "I never saw this Cane."

"I saw him. He has a scar high up on his right arm."

The giant pulled up my shirt. They looked at the scar I got when a sword broke during a fencing lesson.

"And there's this," said Cane as he peeled the cover off the bundle. It was the lost portrait of me. I had forgotten all about it.

"There's the proof that he wears the tartan," the bearded man said. "That's the Gour tartan, but no matter. All are banned."

"How would a servant get his picture painted?" the captain asked.

"The old laird's son paints. He paints anyone who will stand still for him," said Cane.

"Where did he get the tartan?"

"He found it in an old chest in the loft above the stable. He was tried for wearing it last year, but the laird got him off."

"All lies," I said. "French artists don't do portraits of servants. Look at the corner where the artist signed it. His name was J. Genet. Right here you can see—," I was then silenced by what I saw. All of them were staring at the name in the corner: J. Gour.

"As I said," Cane turned to look at me. "This John Scott sings songs too."

"We don't care about that," the captain said.

"You will when you hear one."

"Why?"

"Listen," he said. He proceeded to sing:

> *Scotland is low, Scotland is down,*
> *Ruled over by English vermin.*
> *And even the dogs of the English court*
> *Go bow wow wow in German.*

Cane grinned at me, now quite sure of what he was doing. I said nothing. The song was true. I sang those words as an insult to George III and his German House of Hanover. I had sung it to only a few people, all family or friends. The captain turned and glared at me, his face glowing red.

"Take him on board," he said in a voice like ice.

Some men put me into a boat and rowed out to the ship. They took me down to the hold where I saw some of the men who had been in the room with the captain. The ceiling of the hold was so low that I could barely stand up under it. I looked at the men to see if I knew any of them.

"Do any of you know the earl of Gour?" I asked. "I need to prove that I'm his son."

A skinny fellow of about my age, dressed in rags and missing a front tooth came over to me.

"Hoots," he said. "We dinna ken ane of sicca grand hoose would bide wi' poor us."

"You are on my foot," I said.

"Weel, move," he said and shoved me so hard that I sat down. The men around us guffawed at me. I looked up at the grinning face above me. In Kirkaldy, a cad such as he would have to step aside for me. I leaped to my feet and lunged at him.

"Stop them!" someone called. Captain Chase came down as two sailors pulled us apart. He stood before me.

"You are on my ship now. If you make trouble, I'll put you in irons."

The clerk began to call out names. At each name, a man replied, "Here."

When the clerk said "John Scott," I said nothing.

"John Scott," he said again, louder.

The captain came to me.

"Answer when your name is called."

"My name wasn't called, I'm James Gour."

"See this?" He held out a cat o' nine tails, a whip made with pieces of knotted rope. "Next time you fail to answer, I'll use it. And for each time you say, 'Gour,' you get a day in irons."

"John Scott," the clerk called again. I looked at the whip.

"Here," I grunted.

"Louder or—," Captain Chase raised the whip.

"John Scott," said the clerk again.

"Here!" I yelled so loud that the captain stepped back. Then he went above. The men in the hold had stopped laughing. One, a clean, quiet fellow of about twenty-five, came to me.

"Take care. I've heard tales of these ships."

"What kind of ship is this? Where are we going?"

"To the colonies. These men be bond servants."

"Are they sending me to prison?"

"To work. The captain will sell ye to get back the cost of the trip."

"Sell? To whom?"

"A farmer, maybe. He will buy ye and work ye."

"How long?"

"Four or five years. A lad like ye, 'til ye are twenty-one."

"Twenty-one? No. That would be six years," I said.

I, the son of an earl, to be sold for a slave—it was beyond belief. I sat down on a timber and stared at the floor.

Chapter Five

Rob Graham

LATE IN THE DAY, we were allowed to go up on deck for a while. As we watched the crew make ready to sail, we saw a shore boat come out. A man at each end of the boat rowed while a gentleman sat in the middle. The gentleman wore a lace shirt under his coat of broadcloth which had buttons of gold. As he came on board, a man near me saw him.

"That's Thomas Taggart, the laird who stole the tax money."

The captain met Taggart at the rail. "I'd be honored to have you share my cabin and table," he said.

"He steals twenty thousand pounds and eats with the captain. I steal a cap and I rot below deck," said one of the men with me.

The next morning, I saw what he meant. For breakfast, we got some gruel, like oats cooked black. Two men set a wooden tub down in the middle of the floor and gave each of us a spoon. The men in rags ate like wild beasts, and the fast eaters got most of the food. Late that day, more food was sent down. Each man got a small piece of dry, salted beef with some bread.

"Cap'n is out to gain by starving us," a man said.

After we had eaten our beef and bread, the man who had spoken to me the day before sat down by me. He said his name was Rob Graham. He told me why he was leaving Scotland.

"I was a crofter," he said. "They doubled my rent. The price of cattle went down and the cost of grain to feed them went up."

"Why?"

"A still owner can pay more for grain than I can. Whiskey is worth more than beef."

"Will you be a bond servant to pay for the trip?"

"No. I sold my cattle and paid my debts and my passage. I get head rights for land in the colonies. I dinna want to go, but what can I do?"

"Do you have a family?"

"No more. My wife died last year. Buried in the kirkyard with her father and mother. That's no to be for me."

He looked sad; then he pulled his face into a smile and said, "It's a new land we go to. Belike things are better there."

"It can't be for me," I said. I told Rob who I was and how I got there. He listened. But did he believe me?

Each day, the clerk called to the roll to see if anyone was sick. One day, after the call, he asked me if I could write my name.

"Of course," I said.

"Sign this," he said, holding a paper.

I took it from him and read it.

> *This indenture made and witnessed, that* <u>*John Scott*</u> *hath of his own free and voluntary will placed and bound himself Apprentice unto* _____ _____ *of* _____ *for* _____ *years in payment for his passage to the colonies.*

There was a place for my signature and for witnesses to sign. Rob Graham came over to us.

"How many years?" he asked.

"That will be set at the sale," the clerk said.

"No one should have to sign until he knows how long," Rob said.

"Tell the captain I won't sign," I said.

The clerk went above and came back with the captain.

"What's wrong?" asked the captain, holding his whip where I could see it.

"Why do I have to sign a paper? What about them?" I nodded to the other men in the hold.

"They signed on shore. You didn't. You owe us. If you don't sign, you don't eat."

I had been hungry ever since I got on the ship. I knew I must sign, but first I would haggle.

"How many years?" I asked.

"How old are you?" the captain asked.

"Eighteen," said Graham.

I almost said fifteen, but I realized that if I was to be a slave until I was twenty-one, it would pay to be older. I was glad that I was tall.

"He doesn't look eighteen. Make it five years," the captain said.

I complained, then signed. After all, Rob had saved me a full year of slavery. As I wrote my name on the paper, I again saw the words "my own free will." Parson West said there was no such thing. Maybe he was right.

"I try to be an honest man," Rob said after the captain and clerk were gone. "But it's not right for them to take ye that way."

He had believed me. If only I could make a judge believe it.

"Why did I have to sign a paper if prisoners have no rights?" I asked.

"I am no lawyer," Rob said.

"Maybe he knows that I am by law no prisoner. He would need papers to protect himself."

"Aye," said Rob. "That is it. I've heard of men who kidnap boys and sell them to captains. The man who sold ye must have been a spirit. That's what they call the agents that sell people."

"Why don't the courts stop it?" I asked.

"There's nobody to prove it after the ship leaves."

Nobody to prove it. Would there be a postal service where we were going? I asked Rob if I could write home.

"Ye might if ye had paper, a quill, and money."

All seemed hopeless. It took enough effort just to stay alive. We had to fight for food to survive. One morning, when the gruel was brought down and the men were about to grab for it, Rob raised a hand.

"Wait. Will ye no eat like men than beasts?"

He asked the sailor to go back and get enough cups for us to give each man a cup. Some of the men agreed to that, but one tall man named Till said no. He was one of those that clawed and grabbed at the food before him until it was all gone.

"Who would measure?" he asked.

"Each man will get his turn," said Rob. "But he that measures must take the last cup."

"A man needs more than a boy," Till said, looking at me.

"We will share," Rob said.

The sailor came back with the cups and Rob filled them. Before Till could grab a cup, Rob raised his hand again.

"We give thanks, God, for Thy bounty and put our trust in Thee."

"Bounty," grunted Till as he reached for a cup. But the men ate more slowly. After that, our meals seemed more filling.

As I got to know some of the men in the hold, I found one who knew the bearded man who took me to Captain Chase.

"That be Sam Lynch."

It was the same man that my father sent to prison for stealing. He must have escaped. The long hair tucked into his collar hid the scar on his neck. He had revenge on Father now. And a money pouch full of rents to boot.

One day, while on deck, I asked a sailor where we were going. He kept pulling on the line he held as if I wasn't there. After that, it became a game for me to ask a sailor each day. They all said nothing. Then, one day, a young English sailor talked.

"Where?" he said with a hard laugh. He spit between his teeth and watched the bright fleck sail over the rail and down into the rising sea.

"Why do you want to know?" He laughed again.

"Wouldn't you want to know?"

"Not if I was you. But you asked. We go to a hard land in the New World. We land at a cape there."

"What cape?"

"You are as nosy as Lot's wife."

"Does the cape have a name?" I asked.

"Name? Of course it has a name. They call it the Cape of Fear."

Chapter Six

Bound Over

THE SHIP STOPPED MOVING.

"Let us give thanks," Rob said.

Yes, we had won our fight to stay alive. Seventeen weak men clung to life in the hold, all that were left of the twenty-six who left Scotland. The others had been buried at sea. The dead men were sewed into their blankets and pushed overboard from the swaying ship as Rob said a prayer for them and for us.

Sickness came in all sorts of ways; in the running sea, in bad food, and in smallpox. The worst was the smallpox. After the first case, sailors got lime and spread it around below deck. Lime dust stung our noses and made our eyes water, but it didn't stop the smallpox. It was easy to see why none of the sailors got it. Each one had the marks of that disease on his face. I escaped it, perhaps because I had had cowpox as a child.

In mid-ocean, we met a storm. The raging gray-green sea came at the ship and sent water into the cracks of the deck boards and onto us below. The salty spray helped heal the sores we got from the hard floor. At the worst point of the storm, we got no sleep because of the roll of the ship.

Because we were near land, we hoped for better food. For a week, the servings had been more ample.

"They knew then that they had enough food to last," I said to Rob.

"No," he said. "A fat calf sells better than a thin one."

"A fat calf?" I asked, then I understood what he meant.

We went on deck. A sandy spit of land lay across the bow of the ship; then we moved into the mouth of a river. Some shore boats came out to meet us. The first boat carried just one man to shore, the gentleman Thomas Taggart. The second boat took Rob and the few others who had paid for their passage. When Rob got into that boat, I felt more alone than I had at any time since the night in Edinburgh. But I had no time to dwell on that. The clerk took the rest of us, all to be bond servants, ashore and marched us to a building. A judge there talked to us about our duties and our rights—mostly duties.

"You will be whipped when such is due you," he said. From his tone, it seemed a sure thing that we would need it.

"If you so much as set a hand on your master, you will be tried for treason against the Crown. You will pay for that on the rope, hanged by the neck until dead."

He looked at each of us to see if we got what he said.

"If you leave your master's estate, you must have a pass. Any free man can ask to see it. You may marry only if your master allows you. And if you run away, you will be caught. For that, you will earn a longer term. Are there any questions?"

I stepped forward.

"Yes?" said the judge.

"I'm James Gour, son of the earl of Gour."

At my words, there was a hush for an instant; then all in the room looked at me. One man made a choking sound and the room exploded with laughter. The judge raised his hand.

"Who is this fool?"

"His name is John Scott," said the ship's clerk. He handed a sheet of paper to the judge. The judge read it.

"Bare his right arm," he said.

Before anyone could touch me, I pulled aside my ragged shirt and showed him my scar.

"This signed paper from Tom Cane—," he began.

"A liar," I said.

"Order," he said. Two men came and stood on each side of me.

"Hold your tongue. The paper shows you are John Scott. Amen."

Silent, done for, I felt sick; my name was gone forever. After the hearing, an agent went to the ship's clerk to buy us. I was the last one to be sold.

"This one isn't worth much," the agent said, looking at me. "Seems like a trouble-maker."

"He's strong and fit," said the clerk.

"Look at those hands. Too soft for work."

"Give him a taste of the whip and he'll do wonders," said the clerk.

"I might take him if the price is right. Three pounds."

That was about half his first offer for the others. The clerk shook his head.

"Not enough. But I'll cut the price some if you will take him to the hill country. That's a good place for him." He winked at the agent.

"Then three pounds is enough. That's a long way."

"He's good for five years. Make a sober offer."

They talked a while longer and finally agreed on four pounds. Then the clerk said, "Don't forget—the hill country."

Why did the clerk insist on the hill country? The agent paid the clerk and led us into a street where two Scots were speaking Gaelic.

"Welcome to Notah Kaleena," one said as he looked at the other and grinned. Notah Kaleena. I knew a few words of the old tongue. *Notah* meant "north." North what?

It was hot there. It was odd that such a hot place would have north in its name.

We passed an inn where a black man stood by the door. He played music on a box with some strings and he sang songs to get people to stop there. When we passed, he saw us and sang a new song:

Don't stop at the coast,
don't stop at the river,
It's there you get the shakes
and there you get the fever.

We went to the river and got into a longboat run by some men who spoke German. For a few days, we went upstream. We passed large boats going downriver, most of which were loaded with barrels that had black marks on them. I asked one man that spoke English what was in the barrels.

"Tar," he said, "and pitch."

"Where is it going?"

"To the port, then to England. All naval stores for the British Navy."

To England! Such odd words to make me homesick. If I could put a letter into one of those barrels, it might get to Father—if I had paper and if I had ink. How could I get a letter into the barrel? I would watch for a chance.

One day, we stopped at an open place in the pine woods. The soil there was loose and sandy, but black when you stirred it. The agent paid the boatmen; then marched us from farm to farm, looking for buyers.

"Here comes the soul driver," someone would call out as we came to a farm. Many of the farmers spoke with a Scottish burr.

At times, we saw men cutting the bark off of the tall pine trees to get the oil of tar. The agent sold a servant to a man who ran a kiln, an earth oven made from a mound almost as big as a house. Smoke came out of the hole in the top of the mound, and tar emerged from the end of a hollow log in the side of the kiln. The tar went into a barrel that stood in a pit. I asked the agent what made the tar.

"Pinewood burning inside the kiln." he said.

"Why doesn't it burn the tar?"

"The holes in the mound don't let in enough air for that."

The owner heard us and came near. He looked me over.

"How much is this one?"

"I can't sell him. He goes to the Piedmont."

"Too bad. He acts as if he has a head. That's more than I can say for the last one you sold me."

Again, the hill country for me. Why?

At farms where the agent sold a man, the family fed us and gave us a place to sleep in a shed or barn. Many of the houses we saw were crude, but a few were large and well made. As we went northwest, by the sun, we left the flat land we had seen since the coast. As we got into the hills, we found fewer pine trees and more hardwoods, such as oaks.

One day, we stopped at a few houses near a creek. A man who kept a store there told us that a farmer not far away needed a man. The farmer's name was Richard Smith.

We found the Smith place late in the morning. The house was no more than a large hut built of logs with a clay chimney on one end. A woman, hardly more than a girl, sat on a stump near the door, watching a baby crawl in the dirt.

"We're looking for Richard Smith," the agent said.

The woman got up without a word. She picked up the baby, which began to cry, and went inside. The baby cried louder. A second tot, perhaps two years old, came to the door. The baby screamed and gasped for air somewhere within the dark room.

"Shut up," a man yelled as he came out.

He was older than the woman, almost middle-aged. He had a mop of thick hair and a belly that hung over his belt. His face was coarse with eyebrows that nearly met over his nose. A large dimple over each brow made him appear to be frowning all the time. He pushed the hair back from his bloodshot eyes as if to clear his head of sleep.

"They tell me you need a servant," said the agent.

Smith looked at me as if I smelled bad.

"Him?" he said. "How much?"

"Ten pounds," said the agent.

"Don't talk rot. Four," Smith said.

"He is almost full-grown and good for five years."

"Five years? I'll give you four pounds, six; but I don't like his looks."

"So don't look at him. Work him. He is my last one, so I'll cut the price to seven."

"The last is always the worst. He looks soft—not worth more than five."

They haggled over a price until they agreed on six pounds and a shilling. We went back to the place by the creek to find a justice of the peace. The agent filled in my bond paper and Smith signed it with an X. The agent agreed to file a record at Hillsboro.

When the papers were done, Smith got a jug of spirits from the store and we went back to his farm. He took me to a small shed behind the house.

"You can live here with Scales," he said.

Scales, I found out, was also a bond servant. He had been convicted of stealing a clock in England, and shipped off to be sold.

Smith took me back to the house where he gave me some clothing made of flax. The tow shirt was rough to my skin.

"What about shoes?" I asked. My feet were sore from the long trip.

"You won't need shoes until frost," he said.

"Where do I keep these things?"

He went into the house and came back with three nails.

"Drive these into the wall. Don't come asking for more."

I got a hammer from the tool shed, a tiny room that held two axes, a long saw, some iron wedges, a spade, two long knives, some shears, hoes, and a large iron kettle. When I went back to the hut, I found a chicken inside scratching in the dirt floor. The door was shut, so the hen must have come in through the window. There was no way to close it. I would have looked for some slats or tree branches to keep animals out, but, as it turned out, I had no time for that the first week. What kind of man was Scales to live like this?

I drove the nails into the wall and took the hammer back to the tool shed. When I returned to the hut, the hens were inside again. I ran them out and shut the door. I may have shut it too hard, for the old leather hinge at the top of the door broke and the door sagged. I tried to prop it up, but it didn't stay.

"That door like everything here. Like the people too," said a voice. It came from an old, white-headed black man.

"I'm Mose. This is Julius," he said, dipping his head toward a young black man not much older than I. Julius walked with an odd gait, one shoulder rose and fell with each step. I saw that one of his legs was thin and shorter than the other.

"You'll need a gourd," said Mose. "And some shucks to sleep on. They's some in the corn bin."

He looked at Julius, but Julius frowned at me.

"He can get his own shucks," he said, and limped away.

"Don't pay no heed to him," Mose said, and went with me to get the shucks. I piled them loosely along one wall of the hut. Mose found a gourd and cut it out for a cup.

When we went to supper, the Smiths ate in their house, Scales and I ate in the kitchen cabin, and the black slaves ate on the kitchen porch. There were three black slaves—the two men and an old woman named Maud who did the cooking. The two black men lived in a hut not far from the one Scales and I would share. Maud slept in the loft above the kitchen.

I didn't see Scales until supper. He was a year or more older than I, but no larger. His face looked like an unwashed potato.

After I had met all of them, I saw that each of us had a defect. Mose and Maud were old. Julius was lame. Scales was a shifty-eyed thief, and I had been called a troublemaker. I knew now what Mose meant when he saw the broken door and said, "Like the people too."

After weeks of travel, I finally had a home.

Chapter Seven

Bond Servant

ON MY FIRST FULL DAY at the Smith place, we were called out before daylight to eat a meal of fat bacon and cornbread. Smith took Scales and me to a field of maize that he called corn. Corn in Scotland was a small grain. He gave us long knives and told us to chop the corn. He showed me how to set the stalks into shocks; then he went away.

As I chopped at the tough stalks, my right hand puffed out with blisters. One by one, each blister broke and made a sore. It was September, they said, but the sun was hotter here than any July sun in Scotland. I was still weak from the time on the ship, so I was glad when Scales came to speak to me. He had been working at the far end of the field, and he wanted to change places for a while.

"We take turns," he said. "The woods cut off the air over there, and it's awful hot."

He should be used to the heat, but I wanted to be fair, so I agreed. When I got to his end, I saw that he had cut much less corn than I had. I began to chop, then I heard Smith's voice behind me.

"You are more of a do-nothing than that lazy Scales," he bawled.

He drew a whip from his belt and hit me with it. I put my hand up to save my face.

"Are you raising your hand against me, boy?" he yelled. He grabbed my arms and shoved me against a shock. His

51

face was bent out of shape, and his eyes were glaring. I could smell whiskey on his breath. He shook me again and then pushed so hard that I fell. He hit me again with the whip.

"Now get to work."

I got up and hacked at the corn. I saw Scales bending over, chopping madly.

After Smith had gone, and another hour went by, my head began to ache. The sun was high now and, when I looked across the field, the corn seemed to dance in the heat. I felt sick. Was this a bad dream or was it real? Had I ever been the son of an earl?

Maud brought some food to us, and I went to a tree at Scales' end of the field to eat. My legs almost gave out as I walked. Maud divided the food for us, some potatoes and cornbread with honey. Scales ate without saying a word, looking away at some crows flying above the woods.

"Thanks for the trade," I said.

"I don't feel good today," he said, holding his middle.

"You worked fast when Smith was here."

"I had to. He hates me."

"So you made sure he hates me too."

"Maybe you had a chance in life. I was born to lose."

"Amen, Mr. Scales."

"You think you're better than me."

"No. I know it."

I picked up my knife to go. Scales watched me with a look of pain as if I had hurt him. For my part, the food had revived me a bit. As I worked, I began to think of revenge. If I could survive five years of this, I would be free and get 50 acres of land. I could sell the land and use the money to go back to Scotland. There, as the son of an earl, I would see to my enemies, from Sam Lynch to Richard Smith.

We worked until it was nearly dark and we heard the bell that called us to supper. As I walked from the field, I felt as if I had poison in my veins. After supper, I limped to my hut and discovered that the hens had been there. My bed

shucks were spread all over the floor. Worse still, the hens
had left their droppings in them. The odor would have
been too much for me, but I was too exhausted to get more
shucks. Instead, I pushed them into a pile and fell on it.

The night was short, but I dreamed. I saw the old castle,
my father, and Aunt Alice. I saw my mother, who had been
dead for many years, my first nanny, and then, Jennie
Duncan. Jennie was standing in the path where I last saw
her. She had a handful of flowers that she raised to wave at
me as I came back from a long trip. I awoke with a feeling
of joy until I realized what had gotten me up. It was the
wake-up bell. A wave of gloom came over me as I felt the
ache of never seeing home or Jennie again.

Smith took us out again. He left Scales at one end of the
field and came with me to see what I had done.

"I paid dear for you," he said. "You owe me good work."

It seemed that I owed everyone. I felt that Smith was
trying to excuse himself for beating me. In time, I would
find that his moods went from calm to rage at small things.
He was worse after he had been away to get whiskey or
other spirits.

Smith kept hogs that ran loose in the woods. He cut
notches in the ears of each one to claim them as his. The
hogs went out by day, but came back to their pen at night.
In the fall, after the frost, we killed one for meat. We also
killed one in the winter and another in the early spring.
During the warm months, we ate chicken most of the time.

We ate cornbread every day. We ground the corn with a
heavy stone. The stone was tied to the top of a sapling to
help us raise it. We pulled the stone down hard on the corn
that lay in a dent in the top of a stump.

At the first frost, I asked Smith for shoes. He gave me two
flanks of deer hide and two strips of leather. I wrapped the
hides around my feet and tied the thongs around my
ankles. He gave me one pair of stockings for the coldest
weather. I found some rags and put them around the
stockings to prevent my feet from freezing.

By custom, we were to work five and a half days a week, but we often worked more. We never worked on Sundays. If Smith had tried to work us on the Sabbath, a judge could stop him. Of course, he would never have let us go to a judge, but we could have told a parson. Smith knew that. The only assured day of rest we had was Sunday. How I looked forward to each of those blessed days.

When Scales and I were done with the cornfield, Smith put me to work with Mose. Mose and I took axes to a patch of woods beyond the cornfield to cut trees. At the first tree, Mose cut the brush around the oak while I piled the twigs and sprouts. When we were ready, I picked up my axe and drove it into the trunk of the oak.

"Wait," Mose said. "You can let the work make use of you, or you can make use of the work. The work don't care."

"What's wrong?"

"If you fight the axe, it will fight back."

He showed me how to hold the axe handle, where to place my feet, and how to swing. He picked up his axe and told me to watch how he did it. When he used it, the axe moved like a living thing. He worked easily as if all he had to do was aim the blade. I tried a swing and missed the spot I wanted to hit. The axe bounced off of the tree trunk and almost hit my leg.

"Here," Mose said, taking my axe. He ran his finger over the edge of the blade and shook his head. He got out a cow horn, a leather pouch, and a short piece of flat hickory. He took some hog fat from the horn and dabbed it over the rough side of the wood. He put some sand from the pouch in the fat.

"You can't cut wood with a dull axe," he said.

He spit on the blade, then rubbed the stick with the sand on it across the edge. After doing that a few times, he felt the edge again. Each time he felt the edge, he shook his head. At last, he nodded and gave the axe back to me.

"Don't chop rocks," he said.

He showed me how to cut a notch, low down on the side

of the trunk where we wanted a tree to fall. Then we made
a cut on the far side, a little above the first cut. When the
second notch reached the first one, the tree fell where we
had planned.

Cutting trees was heavy work for me until I learned how
to handle the axe. As I grew more sure in my new skill, I
liked this work better than the cornfield.

Mose sang as we worked.

"Easy cut, easy cut, chop it low and it will go." When the
tree was ready to come down, his song was a warning: "Easy
cut and we pray, easy fall and walk away." As the tree came
crashing down, he would say, "One more and we still here."

He told me of the dangers to a tree cutter. A sudden gust
of wind, a hanging strip of wood, or just bad luck could
turn a tree back onto us. Even a clean cut could go wrong.
The top might hit a tree and the trunk may hop back.

As Mose and I worked in the woods, I wondered why only
he and I were sent there.

"Don't Julius or Scales ever do this?" I asked.

"I've seen Scales try," Mose grinned.

"What about Julius?"

"Never."

"Why?"

"Too dangerous."

"Why does Julius have any say?"

"Julius say? No slave has any say." Mose laughed. He
asked, "How long you here for?"

"Five years."

"That's right, Five. How long am I here for?"

"How long?"

"That's right. How long? 'Til I'm dead, that's how long.
But I'm an old man. Maybe three, maybe five years, then
I'm gone. Now how long is Julius here?"

"'Til he's dead?"

"That's right. But Julius not old like me."

"Oh," I said.

So I had been put at tree work because I was worth less to

Smith than Julius. If I was not worth enough with five years of service to go, how would Smith treat me when I had only a year left? I asked Mose.

"When you have a year left? He try to drive you off."

"Drive me off? Why?"

"So he can catch you and add a year to your time. Or maybe he just work you to death. When you got no time left, he don't care."

So, I could expect things to get worse instead of better. I thought of home again. I told Mose about Scotland and the land that Father owned there.

"I'm his only son. If I were there, he would leave it all to me."

"Or you to it."

I had not seen it that way but, on the other hand, I did feel the burden of it when Father told me I must run the land.

"Yes," I said, "but better a rich slave than a poor slave."

"Best no slave," Mose said.

I told Mose about the boats loaded with barrels for England that I saw on the Cape Fear River.

"Maybe I could send a letter to Scotland."

"Who's going to take it?"

"If I ever get to a city with a post service—"

"What post? Maybe in Virginia. We're in Carolina."

Carolina. *Notah Kaleena* the Scot had said. North Carolina.

"There must be some way," I said.

"Always is. If you got money."

"I could promise—"

"Promise. You think a promise can go to Virginia and across water. A promise get mighty thin all that way."

"Then I need money."

"No money here."

Mose was right. If I couldn't prove my name in Scotland, so close to home, how could I do it here? Mose said we were in one of the wildest parts of the colonies that had farm land. No wonder the ship's clerk told the agent to take me to the hill country. Maybe the captain and clerk knew that I was no criminal. But who at home had betrayed me? Who stole the portrait and gave it to Sam Lynch? Who told the song I'd sung about King George? Who hated me that much? I could do nothing about it here. No one here even knew there was an earl of Gour.

Julius came to the woods one morning with a message from Smith. He talked to Mose as if I wasn't there.

"Marstuh wants us all at the shed when the sun is straight up."

"What are we going to do there?" I asked.

"You are a pretty smart man, Scott. You ought to know more than me."

I felt my face grow hot with anger.

"You say more than one with your frame can risk." I said.

"I don't scare from a man who give hisself away for a slave," he said, his lip curling.

"So, that's it." All at once, I saw why Julius had no use for me. "I didn't choose to be a slave any more than you did. They caught me and put me on a ship and brought me to this place. It was sign up or starve."

"Who saying that?"

"I'm saying it."

"You can both stop that talk. No good anyhow," Mose said. "Now what do Marstuh want?" he asked Julius.

"He wants us to go get some pigs he bought and drive them home," Julius said.

A small bird flew by us and landed on a tree branch near us. When it broke into song, it was the loudest I had ever heard from a small bird.

"Joe-reaper, Joe-reaper, Joe-ree," it seemed to say.

"Sound like that bird say 'work harder'," said Mose.

"What kind of bird is it?" I asked.

"A wren. Carolina wren, some say. I've heard tell that that

bird say 'freedom' sometimes. I think I never heard that word, even from a bird."

I said nothing. I was thinking that maybe I would never hear it again either.

Chapter Eight

Class Differences

AFTER I HAD BEEN at Smith's place for a few months, I told him that I wanted to go to church on Sundays.

"Too far," he said. "You'd have to walk ten miles there and back."

"You refuse?"

"Go on then. But don't think that long walk will get you out of any work."

The next Sunday, I walked to Winona, a town of a few houses, a store, and an Anglican church. I got there early, and when I saw that it was the Church of England, I paused. I had never been to one, but I knew that it was that or none.

I went in. No one was about except a boy who was there to ring the bell. He stared at me. I found a pew and waited. Two women and some girls came in. As they came near my pew, one of the girls gasped and clapped a hand over her open mouth. I wondered what was so odd about me.

A group of people came in. One of them was a sharp-faced man dressed in black with black hair except for a ring of white around his ears. He came to my pew and faced me.

"Who are you?" he asked.

"John Scott," I answered, having lost any hope of using my real name.

"Are you bonded?"

"Yes."

"To whom?"

"Richard Smith."

"Smith? No member here. Too bad. I would have you whipped."

"For what?"

"Don't you know that servants don't enter the church until after all the gentlemen's families are in?"

I looked around. No one else wore the clothing of a poor person.

"If you knew who I am—," I began, turning into James Gour again.

"I know who you are. You are a bond servant."

"Have you made God a respecter of persons here?"

"Your words are as bad as your acts. You owe honor to your king. Gentlemen are the king's agents here. Go out and wait your turn."

As I went out, I shut the door with a bang. Someone called my name. It was Rob Graham.

"Where are you now?" he asked. I told him about Smith's farm.

"I have 50 acres of land of my own now. All mine," he said.

"Is life easier for you here than in Scotland?"

"No, not yet."

"Do you miss the highlands?"

"Aye. The bonny highlands. I was poor there too, but back there a man is poor forever. I could never own property there, and if ye have no property, ye have no freedom."

"And none for sure if you are a bond servant like me. A man with white and black hair just gave me a lesson in that."

"That be Reverend Crouch. Did he give ye a warm welcome?"

"He put me out. Until I was fifteen, no man could put me out anywhere."

"Ye were lucky. It's no that way for most—nor for ye now. Will ye stay and worship with us? I am Presbyterian, but we have no such church here."

"Worship? With Crouch?"

"Aye. We can worship God here as well as anywhere, Crouch or no Crouch. Coming to church will make ye feel better."

"I feel worse already."

"Belike Crouch won't be here forever."

"All right," I said. "I'll stay, but someday I'll have revenge on some people. Crouch is one of them."

"Nay, don't be that way. 'Vengeance is mine, saith the Lord.'"

"But if I take revenge, I will see it done. That will be sweet."

"Time passes. So does anger. We can go in now."

Crouch spoke about duty, the duty of a servant toward his master and king. I learned that it was his pet topic. Later that year, Crouch left and a new parson came down from Virginia. He was William Law, a young man with fine features and a neat club haircut. His gray coat made him seem less stiff than Crouch, who always wore black.

People often took dinner to the church, and Law invited me to stay. After dinner, we would talk. One Sunday, I told him that, while I didn't agree with Crouch, I had to admit that a class system was often good.

"Some bond servants are no good," I said, thinking of Scales.

"True. But do you class yourself that way?"

"No, I hope not," I said, wondering if I should tell him my true name.

"I don't know your master; but I would guess that you are as moral as he," said Law.

"That is no great honor. He is one of the worst men I know."

"Then you see how our class order can be bad. I know a man who, like you, wants classes; but he would change who goes to the top. He calls his a natural system."

"What does he mean by that?"

"Your class would be set by virtue instead of birth."

"Who would decide?"

"You would be known by what you do, not by a lucky birth."

"I don't know."

"Tom has other ideas too. He wants to stop the big land grants to rich men. He would like to see many small land owners instead of a few big lords."

"Who is this man?"

"Tom is a member of the Virginia House of Burgesses."

"Tom who?"

"Tom Jefferson. A few years from now, you won't have to ask Tom who. But I should not be for him."

"Why?"

"Tom says it isn't right to tax all the people to support our English church."

"What do you think?"

"I'll tell you some day," he said with a smile.

"I know what Crouch would say. He would be for more taxes if it helped him."

"It's church policy," said Law.

And Law, of course, could not speak against it. I didn't know what he would say if he were free to speak, but I felt sure he didn't see eye-to-eye with Crouch.

One Sunday, Old Parker, the man who read the Bible for Law, said he wanted to quit. Law asked who would like the duty, and I got up. I heard a "tee-hee" and saw people looking at each other with amusement. Law gave no heed to them as he handed me the Bible. I began to read, and those who had laughed a moment before, stared blankly at me in surprise. After that, I read every Sunday.

One Sunday night, Julius came back to the Smith place from a meeting at a neighboring farm where a black preacher known as Old Jim had spoken. The old man told the crowd that all of them should be baptized.

"So will you do it?" Julius asked.

"Why don't you get Old Jim to do it?"

"He's too scared," said Julius, his lip curling.

"Of what?"

"Of Marstuh Smith. He say he won't hear to such a thing for a slave. Old Jim say to obey God but ask Marstuh. Marstuh Smith say no."

Of course he would.

"Well, will you?" Julius asked.

"Why me?"

"I hear tell you can read the Bible. So maybe you know how to baptize me."

"I think you would have to have people around to do what Old Jim is talking about. You want to be baptized and God knows that. Don't you think God judges us by why we do things as much as by what we do?"

"Maybe. That sounds right."

"There was the thief on the cross that didn't get baptized. I guess some people would say that that was a special case, but I say that being a slave is a special case. God doesn't expect you to do what you can't do. No man can rule what you think."

"Amen."

"Maybe someday you will leave Smith."

"Praise God if I do."

"Don't talk to Smith about it again. That won't help."

"I hear you."

Smith wouldn't want us talking like that. He did not like for white servants and black slaves to talk, except at work. He saw skin color as a way to divide us; but when he found that Mose and I worked well together, he gave us more jobs to do.

During the winter, we made things of wood, tables for the house, feed boxes for the pigs, and any other items that Smith wanted. Mose showed me how to use an axe to shape wood. To make a table leg, Mose would saw a block of wood to the right length; then he would split the block this way and that, until he had a piece as thin as he needed. Using the axe blade, he could smooth the rough edges to make a square leg or slice off the corners for a round leg.

As the year of 1774 passed, I saw that Mose had aged since I had come to the Smith farm. During the late winter, Mose became sick. I kept thinking that he would get well when spring came, but spring was late that year. After each effort, Mose would bend over, coughing. One day, I spoke to Smith about it.

"Mose is getting too old to work in the field. Why can't he help Maud in the garden or the kitchen?"

"Maud don't need help."

"But Mose needs easier work."

"He don't earn his keep now. Boy, are you trying to tell me how to run this place? Do your own work. I'll see to Mose."

Later that week, as Mose and I were carrying wood, he fell. I helped him onto a stump.

"Someday, I fall and don't get up," he said, wiping the dampness from his head with a trembling hand. I told him to rest while I moved the wood. Smith came back from Winona and saw our small pile of wood.

"Lazy dog," he said, reaching for his whip. Mose got up and hobbled toward us.

"Don't," he called to Smith. "I...I..."

Mose swayed as he tried to walk. He was trying to talk, but I couldn't tell what he was saying. Maybe he was going to say that he was sick and the low stack of wood was his fault. When Smith saw him, he turned on Mose with the handle of his whip. I looked at the stick of wood in my hand. All at once, an urge hit me to stop Smith with it, but I knew that I might as well strike King George himself.

Mose went down. I don't know if he fell from Smith's blows or because he was sick.

"Get up," Smith yelled. He bent over to look at Mose, then came away.

"Take the old fool to his cabin," he ordered and went to his house.

I looked around for help. Julius, who was grinding corn, came over. We carried Mose to his hut and laid him down.

At supper, Maud gave us some soup to take to Mose, but he couldn't eat. We spoke to him, but he couldn't talk. I got a gourd and went to the well for water. As I neared the hut again, Julius came out. I knew, before he got to me, what he was going to say. Mose was dead.

The next day, we buried Mose on the hill behind the cabins where there were two other graves.

"Lift him down easy, he's had it so hard," Maud said.

I said the Twenty-third Psalm. After we went down the hill, I found a flat piece of stone and, day-by-day, cut at it until I had made the four letters to spell Mose. One night, after work, I took it up to his grave. It was the last thing I could do for my old friend. When I left there, I sat on a stump for a long time, looking at the stars. As I looked out at the points of light in the night sky, an old feeling came over me again. I was alone.

Chapter Nine

McGill

ONE SUNDAY, CROUCH CAME BACK to church for a visit. He asked Law to let him preach the sermon, and I read the Scripture for him. His topic, again, was duty.

"There is a natural order among men," he said. "It makes some men rulers and some servants. This order is of God. If a servant feels that he is ill-used by his master, he has a sure way to better his lot. He can work harder."

As he talked, I saw Thomas Taggart again, the man who stole the tax money. And Captain Chase, ready to lick his boots—even if he was a thief—because he was a rich thief. Then there was Smith, who had killed Mose with hard work, and denied Julius his baptism. Julius was at the mercy of men like Smith and so was I. I had hope of freedom someday; Julius had none. A natural order? Not God's natural order. Not Tom Jefferson's natural order. Crouch's natural order.

After the service, Crouch came to me.

"You read well," he said.

I nodded. What did he want?

"Can you write and do numbers?"

"Yes."

"How long is your term?"

"Four more years." I had been with Smith a year.

"Do you think Mr. Smith would sell your bond?"

"I don't know."

"I am going to be a magistrate, and I need a clerk."

"I see." My heart jumped. As a clerk, there would be no more toil in hot summer sun nor chill in winter snow. Clerks had a good life. I had heard farmers say that it cost as much to have a clerk copy one paper as they could earn on the farm in a month. Of course, as a bond servant, I would get nothing but food and shelter. But after my bond ended, easy money.

"There is a good future for people who can be loyal," he said.

"Loyal?"

"To their masters and to King George."

Something about that made me uneasy.

"You may as well know now that I will demand absolute loyalty," he said. "A good clerk does what he is told and talks to no one. Can you do that?"

"What if a poor man can't pay—"

"You have been talking to the raff. They always howl. Instead, they should work harder."

Work harder. There it was again. Bond servants who were ill-used could work harder. A poor crofter in the highlands who had no money for rent could work harder. It was easy to say.

"What—"

"No. No more questions. How dare you? I can see that you are not the right man for—"

"I don't want to be your clerk."

"And I wouldn't have you. What is more, I shall give your name to every magistrate in the colony. You are a man that needs watching."

I left the church with mixed emotions. Although I had put away a sure path out of Smith's farm, I went back to its hard work easy in my soul. I felt as if I had escaped a snare of Satan. Singing to myself, I went into the woods. Was I crazy? No. I had learned something worth knowing, a way out of slavery. People who could read and write must be needed in this wild place, or Crouch would have never even

considered me. My skill with books would pay off for me
yet. Suddenly, relying on skill made more sense than relying
on a name. Until I was fifteen, the magic of my name was
all that I needed. Now it seemed to be a weak—and easy to
lose—crutch. No more would I hope to get someone to help
me just because I was the son of an earl. No more. If I was
to be free, I had to do it myself.

Later that year, a new family joined the church, some
Scots named McGill. One Sunday, after church, McGill
came to me.

"I heard ye read. How much education have ye?"

"Enough," I said.

"Can ye do numbers and writing?"

"Yes."

"Can you teach that to a child?"

"In time."

"How many years are ye bound for?"

"Four more."

"How much could ye teach children in four years?"

"Reading, writing, and numbers up to the rule of three."

"Would ye like to do that if I bought ye?"

"Yes, if I could be free as soon as your children can read,
write, and do numbers."

"I will see," he said.

Again, I had some hope. McGill would be sure to try to
find a cheaper way to educate his children, but there were
no schools nearby. He would surely have to come back to
me. Next time, I might ask for more than freedom.

The next week, McGill came to see Smith. He stopped at
the field where I was digging sprouts.

"Are ye ready to teach my children?" he asked.

"Yes," I said. "But I want my freedom as soon as they can
read, write, and do numbers. And I want a good suit of
clothes."

"What aboot head rights?"

"I want my head rights."

"How much did Smith pay for ye?"

"Six pounds and a shilling."

"For six pounds, I can do that."

Smith came to the field. He frowned at us.

"Would ye sell this laddie?" McGill asked.

"No. I've lost one boy. Only got three left," said Smith, shaking his head.

"I'll give ye six pounds for him."

"No. Not six nor sixteen pounds."

McGill went to his horse.

"Let me know if ye change on it," he said and rode away.

Smith faced me with a sour look.

"Why does he want you?" he asked.

"I met him at church. He asked who held my bond."

"That's no answer, boy. Why did he offer six pounds? Have you been talking my business around?"

"Well you know now where to find a buyer if you do ever want to sell me. I thought you would like that."

"You think too much, boy. I'll do the thinking on this place. Your job is to get these sprouts out of this field."

I began digging again. When I looked out over the field, it seemed to go on forever.

Chapter Ten

The Smoking Fire

SMITH, LIKE MOST FARMERS I knew, did nothing to save the soil on his farm. Land was cheap, so if a man wanted better crops, he moved. Mose had told me that our crops grew weaker by the year, and I could see that he was right. The vegetable garden, on an acre of poor soil, was the worst. One day, I saw Smith looking at it.

"Why don't we put manure on the ground?" I asked.

"Manure?" he said, his mouth open as if he didn't trust what he had heard.

"The plants are pale. They need feeding. Manure—"

"Manure? We eat potatoes and beans from there."

"People in Scotland do too, but they use manure."

"This ain't Scotland. You keep that manure out of my garden."

I was sure that I could grow better crops and more kinds of food than Smith. We added to our diet with wild fruit and berries. I would have planted tame ones. We got a change in meats when Smith shot game such as rabbits, deer, and turkey—but he often only got enough for his family.

In my second year on the farm, it was dry. By early July, the tops of the corn leaves had turned brown. In the fall, we got only half a crop. Farmers in the bottoms, along the creeks, had corn. Smith could buy corn from them, but where would he get the money? One Sunday, I found out where he planned to get the money. He went to church with me, and when we got there, he talked to McGill. The next day, McGill came to Smith's place, bringing some men with him. Smith put his mark to a paper, McGill gave him some money, then Smith told me to go with McGill.

McGill's farm was a big change for me. His house, which was made of bricks, set in the center of a yard that was rimmed by a stone wall. Behind the house was a brick kitchen; and behind that were some cabins. McGill showed me around and gave me a cabin—a home as good as the one Smith lived in. McGill also gave me an old suit of clothes.

"Ye are a schoolmaster now," he said. "What will ye need?"

"Books and paper," I said.

"Aye. And shoes." He was looking at my bare feet.

The next day, we saddled two horses and went to Hillsboro. We took a notch road, a lane marked by notches on the trees to show the way. At the town, we stopped at an inn, a two-story building with porches upstairs and down. When we ate there the next morning, I felt like a gentleman again.

We found a store that was run by a man with a Scottish burr to his speech. He showed me some shoes. "My best," he said. We asked the price.

"A pound, two shillings, and five pence."

"Too much," McGill said.

"Oh. Ye want cheap shoes?"

"Not cheap. Sensible."

I watched the two Scots each try to get the best of the deal. The trader got out another pair of shoes.

"These are a pound, a shilling, and four pence."

"I'll give ye a pound and a shilling," McGill said.

The other man looked at the shoes.

"Canna do that. But give me two pence extra."

McGill agreed. They made each deal the same way, the store man setting the price and McGill making a lower bid.

When we had all the things we needed there, we went to a blacksmith shop to get some tools. McGill gave the smith an order for the iron work he needed and left. He told me to wait at the shop if I wanted to. I sat on a keg for a while and then went to see the town.

As I walked down the street, I heard people talking about King George. Men from the hills, on foot with skinny dogs at their heels, had no use for a king. Others, in good suits, talked about loyalty.

I came to an empty lot where a man stood on a stump and spoke in a loud voice to a small crowd. He was not a handsome man, but it was easy to see that he could hold the crowd in his hand. He was not tall, but he seemed tall. He had a large nose, brown hair, and sloping shoulders. His speech had a hint of Scotland in it.

"Who is that?" I asked.

"John Witherspoon," said a man in front of me.

"No freedom," Witherspoon was saying. "The bishops of the Anglican Church can see no wrong in the head of their church, King George. They refuse every one of our calls for justice, and yet they expect you to pay taxes to help them."

When Witherspoon was done, the men around me began to argue about what he had said.

"He's from New Jersey," said one man. "Some place called Princeton. He's president of a college there."

"Yes," said a shop owner. "Of course a man from there is against England. The English have stopped trade with them, but not with us. England has been fair with North Carolina."

"Fair with us. But why?" asked another man.

"To get our naval stores," said a third. "They need our tar, our oil of tar, and our tall pines for their ships. They think they can run over us and still get them. I say no."

"You hill country Irish are always against King George," the shop man said.

"We're no Irish."

"I know you Sam Corbett. You were born in Ireland, and if that don't make you Irish—"

"Belike if I was born in a barn, I'd be a horse?"

"They call you Scotch-Irish. Maybe you're just part Irish."

"They call us that, but we are no Irish. We are Scots who lived in Ireland for a while. And none of us take to King George."

"You Scotch-Irish are the black sheep of the empire. You seem to feel that when you find a place with no fights, it is your duty to start one. You break every law—"

"We keep God's laws."

"And every other good thing you can get your hands on."

I saw Witherspoon walking away, so I ran and stopped him.

"So you run a college?" I asked.

"Aye. Would ye want to go there?"

"Not yet," I said. "What kind of subjects does your college teach?"

"All of the usual, but I have added some, such as History, French, and Philosophy."

"Are you from Scotland?" I asked.

"Aye. Born there and preached there."

"So you are a parson?"

"Aye. But my talk here is no preaching. I try not to put words in my sermons that will set people at odds, but we must have freedom. A man must be able to worship God as he sees fit. There are good people on each side, but freedom will come."

I went back to the shop and talked to the smith who was making the tools for McGill. I asked him if the Scotch-Irish were the only people there who were against King George.

"Oh no. They are more so than some, but the longer a man has lived here, the more against the king he will be—unless he is on the royal payroll."

"What about the women?"

"Most believe like their men. My wife does. We worked a

piece of ground for ten years, then we lost it to a crooked sheriff."

"How?"

"He set the taxes and said he'd give me time to get the money. But he sold me out afore I could reach town. There's no money here. London keeps it all so the king's agents can prosper on us."

"You lost your farm. Couldn't you go to court?"

"It would take a month's work to pay for five minutes' time of the clerk and a summer to hire a lawyer. They wouldn't show me the law books that set the fees. All are set up to rob the farmer."

"What about the assembly? Could it help you?"

"Not while Fanning sat in it. To show what he did, he got double fees, so they fined him. Guess how much?"

"I have no idea."

"No, you don't. A penny. They fined him a penny. For me, it would be irons. We elected Husband in place of Fanning. He asked for things we needed."

"What kind of things?"

"Salaries for clerks instead of fees. The right to small claims without a lawyer. And an end to them big land grants."

So, some of Tom Jefferson's plans were spreading.

"If they will treat us right, we can be just as loyal as any Englishman," the smith said. "People in England are like the elder sons. They get it all. We're the younger sons. We get nothing."

McGill came back, and we left for home. I rode behind McGill, thinking about the things I'd heard in town. When John Witherspoon said that liberty would come, it was easy to believe him. But how could these people fight the British empire? I recalled a fire in the woods the year before. Mose and I had burned some brush near an old stump, but we thought that the fire was out. We made a new pile of brush around the stump, planning to burn it later. One day, I saw a bit of smoke near the pile, then it was gone. The next day, as we worked nearby, the pile burst into flames. The fire must have been there in the old stump all the time. What I had heard in Hillsboro was like the fire that slept in the stump. When would the fire of revolt against King George break out in these colonies?

Chapter Eleven

The Mark of Traitor

ON THE FOLLOWING SUNDAY, when we went to church, McGill took me to meet his friends.

"This is Mr. Scott, our tutor," he said even to people that I knew before McGill had come to Carolina.

As I read the Scripture for Law in my suit and new shoes, I saw McGill looking around to see how people liked his tutor. While I was reading, Crouch came in. At the end of the service, he asked to speak.

"I have come to warn of traitors," Crouch said. "We know that mob rule has been attempted before in this colony."

He was referring to the days of the Stamp Act. I had heard about it. A crowd took over the ship of stamps from England. They went to the governor's mansion and forced the stamp master to sign an oath not to sell stamps.

"The stamp protest was a case of mob rule," Crouch said again, "like the riff-raff of Boston."

We had heard about the Boston Tea Party.

"Tea is a good thing," Crouch said. "Some people don't drink it now. They are wrong. I hope that none of you are like that."

He looked at me.

"Do you drink tea?" he asked.

He was trying to mark me as a traitor. Those who sold or drank tea called it the "loyal drink." To others, it was the "East Indian Brew."

"Well, do you?" he asked again. "We are waiting for your answer."

"No," I said.

I heard a murmur in the pews.

"No," I said again. "I was a bond servant to Richard Smith, and at Smith's it was water in a gourd for me."

Someone giggled and, at that, a titter went through the crowd.

"Can you pray for King George?" Crouch asked me.

"I can pray for his soul," I said.

"Can you pray for the success of his loyal men against the scum of these colonies?"

"I can pray for his soul."

"You are a traitor," Crouch said. He picked up a Bible. "We all know that true religion makes a man loyal to his king. Kings are ordained by God. King George was meant to rule us. It is a sin for you to fail him."

"What about King Herod?" I asked. "The king who killed John the Baptist and wanted to kill Jesus. Was it wrong to fail him?"

Crouch put the Bible down and marched to the back of the church. He stopped and shouted at us.

"I refuse to be insulted anymore by this...this cur of low degree. If you keep him in your church, he will rot it. I have some things to say to the warden of the vestry."

After Crouch had gone, some men of the church asked Law for a meeting. I saw them talking to Law and looking at me as they spoke. Law came to me.

"They want a word with you," he said. "I may be asked to remove you as reader."

I nodded. We joined the men who had been talking to him.

"As I told these gentlemen, I think Crouch is wrong to put politics in the service," Law said to me so the others could hear. "But you might better have said nothing."

"But Crouch made him speak on the tea," said Rob Graham. "And Crouch is no a parson now."

"No, but he was ordained in England, so he can speak for the church," said Law. "He has King George and his agents behind him."

"Yes, but not forever," I said.

"Don't talk treason," said a man named Frazier.

"I looked at each group of the men in the group. Most of them were Scots: Ross, Frazier, and Campbell. McGill sat in a pew behind them, looking at the floor.

"Are you Scots really for King George?" I asked.

"Aye," Frazier said. "We have to be loyal. I have a father, a mother, and two brothers in Scotland."

"We fear for our kin," said Ross.

"And some of us draw a pension from the crown," said Frazier.

"Have you forgotten what the English did to our men after 1745?" I asked.

"It's a long time since Culloden," one said.

"We don't want another such war," said Brian Campbell.

"No wonder you feel that way," I said. "The Campbells went with the English to fight our Scots."

"Ye are far too young to know about all that. Even some families were divided by the war."

"Aye," said another. "The brother of the earl of Gour went with the English. Some say that such brothers did that so the family could keep their land no matter who won."

"That wasn't true of the Gours," I said in sudden anger.

"Oh no? And what do you know of the Gours?"

That came from Allan Ross, a middle-aged farmer. All at once, they seemed to be staring at me. I looked at Ross. Had I seen him before?"

"I've heard of the Gours," I said. A year before, I would have told all, but never again would I claim my name without proof.

"So ye've heard of the Gours?" said Ross. "Then maybe ye had heard how the brother got all of the land in the end, after the old Laird died last year. What's wrong?"

I had turned away from them.

"What happened to the earl's son?" I asked.

"Ran off to be an artist. Took some money and went. Did ye know him?"

"When we were young," I said.

My father died thinking that I had taken the rents. I went out of the church and waited for McGill. When the meeting ended, he came out and we rode home.

"I won't have a servant who goes against King George," he said. "I served him in the army. I am on half pay now. I can't take his money and let you do that."

"A man must think for himself," I said.

"Unless he be a servant."

"When your children are done, I will no longer be a servant."

"That will be almost four more years."

"What of our talk that I can be free when the children are educated?"

"That was if I got ye for six pounds."

"How much did you pay?"

"More."

"How much more?"

"A servant needn't know the master's affairs."

"I still think that if Crouch is for King George, I am not."

"Would ye want to go back to digging roots and chopping wood?"

"No."

"Then be quiet. Don't talk treason."

And so I said no more. I worked with McGill's children that winter and through the next summer and fall. Another year had passed, leaving three more to go. As the new year of 1776 arrived, I wished, as I had the year before, that it could be my last year as a servant. It was always a hope, but a dim one.

The days went by, one much like another, until one afternoon in early February. One of McGill's black slaves came to me where I was working with the children, two boys and a girl. He said a man was looking for me and was at my cabin now. As soon as I ended the lessons, I went to the cabin. It was Scales.

"I need help," he said, his face screwed into a look of pain.

"Are you hurt?"

"No, it's worse than that."

I saw then that it was not pain, but fear on his face.

"What have you done?" I asked.

"It wasn't me. If you don't help me, they'll hang me."

"What happened?"

"I was cutting wood—," he started.

As he said that, I knew why he had to cut wood now. With Mose dead and me gone, Smith had no one else to do it. Julius, of course, was worth too much for that job.

"A hunter came out of the woods with a dog and a gun. Smith came along—and he had been at the whiskey—and he told the man to keep his dog off his land. The man said his dog would go anywhere it wanted to go. Smith grabbed the man's gun and shot the dog; then the man took the axe from me and hit Smith with it. They'll hang me."

"Do you know the man who did it?"

"Never saw him before. Smith's woman heard the shot and came out. The man told her that I killed Smith. He said he took the axe away from me."

"Did anybody see the man hit Smith?"

"Nobody but Julius, and his word won't count."

That, I knew, was true.

"You've got to help me, or they'll hang me." He was almost crying now.

"You would never help me."

"Are you going to let them kill me?" His voice broke.

"Why should I believe you?"

"I've been a liar and I've been a thief, but I ain't never been a killer."

The way he said it sounded true.

"Why did you come to me?" I asked.

"Where else can I go? If you don't help me, they'll hang

me. But it ain't really for killing Smith, even if I had killed him. It's for the things I stole in London. That's why I'm here. When they send you as a servant, they take away all of your rights."

"Sit down and stop crying," I said.

"I'll pay you back any way that I can," he said.

"I owe you nothing, but I don't want to see you hanged."

I got some paper and wrote two notes for him.

"Look at this word, P-A-S-S. That means pass. Show it to anyone who stops you. I've signed McGill's name to it. The other paper is a letter to John Williams in Philadelphia. I don't know any such man, but you can say you're taking it to him. Go north to Virginia and keep going north—and stay out of trouble."

I got some food from the kitchen for him, and he left as soon as it was dark. I expected to hear of Smith's death but I did not. I thought that someone would be looking for Scales, but for the next few days, there was no one. I was sure that Scales had made his escape.

One day, I was called out into the yard by McGill. He was talking to a man whose back was turned to me.

"Here he is now," McGill said when he saw me.

The man turned. As he did, I stumbled and almost fell. It was Richard Smith.

Chapter Twelve

A Winter Walk

"HAVE YOU SEEN SCALES?"

It was what I knew Smith would ask, but I had no answer. Instead, I spoke to McGill.

"Scales is a bond servant to Mr. Smith," I said.

"He knows that. Why do you think I am here?" said Smith. "I am looking for Scales. Where is he?"

"I don't know. He isn't here," I said.

"No," said McGill.

That word from McGill was enough. Smith turned to go, and I saw a strip of cloth under his hat.

"What is wrong with your head?" I asked.

"Mind your own head," he said and left.

As I worked with the McGill children that day, I went over, again and again, the story that Scales had told me. His panic had been real, but he could have lied about the details. Even if he had done nothing more than hit Smith, Scales could be hanged. No wonder his voice had the ring of truth when he said he wasn't a killer. Smith was alive. And Scales must have known that. Why did I believe him at all?

About a week later, a sheriff brought Scales to the McGill place. McGill sent for me and faced me with the pass.

"This man says ye did this."

"Yes. I wrote it."

"Why?"

I told him the story that Scales had told me.

"Ye signed my name. That won't do."

"No."

"I warned ye."

"Yes."

"Ye will be sold."

That was all. What would be the charge against Scales? If it was for running away, he would get more time on his bond—but so would I. And if for treason?

What should I do? When I asked myself that question, I remembered what happened that night in Scotland. I stood on a step in a dark street and did nothing. That was my last chance to escape. This time, I would not wait.

I got some paper and wrote a pass. Instead of putting McGill's name on it, I made up a name for my master. It was Daniel Clark of Richmond, Virginia. For my own name, I wrote John Freeman. I got some food from the kitchen when the cook was out. At dark, I put on the long, wool great coat that McGill had given me and I left.

Which way? Scales had gone north and was found, so I would go south. I looked at the stars to find the pole star. With it behind me, I ran for the first mile or more; then I walked at a steady pace. The night was cold but still. Sometimes I heard a dog bark. At the sound, I turned right or left until I got around the danger.

When I saw the sky growing light in the east, I left the high ground and found a creek. I went along it until I found a field with some shocks of corn left standing. I saw smoke in the valley across the creek; that would be the nearest cabin. I dug into one of the corn shocks, pushing out the stalks to make room inside. I ate some of the cornbread and pork that I took from the kitchen, and curled up with dry corn blades under me. The hole in the shock soon became warm. As I was thinking what a cozy place I had found, I went to sleep.

A dog barked. I half woke and tried to go to sleep again, but the barking got louder. I peeped through the stalks and saw a brown dog with long floppy ears. He jumped back and forth as he barked just outside the shock. When I looked past the dog, I saw some men moving across the field. One of them broke away from the others and ran toward me. The dog barked faster and came closer to the shock, his muzzle almost touching the stalks. The man came up to the dog and jabbed a gun into the shock, hitting me.

"Something in there," he said, as if to the dog.

The other men stopped and watched.

"Something here," the man called to the others.

At that, I crawled out. I saw that the men were all dressed alike, with cocked hats and tan knee breeches. Each man wore a pack on his back, and they all had guns. A man with small white cuffs on his sleeves came away from the others to meet me.

"What say you of King George?" he asked.

"Who are you?" I asked.

"Never mind that. What say you of King George?"

"I say down with those lords over the sea." I wondered, will I be shot? Or arrested? Instead, a cheer went up.

"Come and help us save Cape Fear from the Tories," one said.

"Find him a gun, sergeant," said another.

"In time," said the man with the white cuffs. He was a tall man, about thirty years old. Most of the other men were younger than he. One, a thin blond lad with freckles, looked to be my age or even younger.

"Who are you?" the sergeant asked.

"John Scott. Bond servant to a Tory."

"He'll make a good rebel," someone said.

"Can I go with you?" I asked.

"For now, at least," said the sergeant.

"Good."

And so I moved on with the little army. As we hiked along, I fell in with the youngest one. He said his name was Hugh Gordon. Hugh told me about far off events, of battles at Lexington and Concord, and of other events closer to home.

"Some folks right here in North Carolina are asking for independence," he said. "One county has a declaration, they say, and people say no to them offices and other honors to men of high birth."

There was Tom Jefferson's philosophy again.

"We want county records open to all," another man said.

"Josiah Martin, the British governor, has asked for redcoats to join with the Tories to hold the colony for the Crown," said Hugh.

"Who is against the Tories?" I asked.

"Farmers mostly, except for the big planters, and anybody who doesn't want a king. A lot of people everywhere, but less in one county, Cumberland."

"Cumberland County? Who named it?"

"Must have been the Scots. It's full of Scots."

"They named their county for Butcher Cumberland? I can't believe it."

"Butcher Cumberland? Who's that?"

"He was the uncle of George III. He gave death to two thousand Scot prisoners after Culloden in 1745. We named a flower after him. Stinking Billy."

"Are you a Scot?"

'Yes. I can't believe that many Scots would fight for King George," I said.

"They are raising an army. That's why we are marching."

"Down with the Scots," said a man in front of me.

"Halt," yelled the leader. He came back to us.

"Who said that?"

"I did," the man said in a low voice.

"What's your name?"

"Wilson."

"Well, Wilson, so you don't like the Scots. What are you?"

"English."

"English? Then maybe you should join the Tories."

"The Tories?"

"That's right. We don't need any English here. We don't need Scots, Irish, or Germans either."

A murmur went through the crowd. One man said, "They don't want you, Kelly."

He replied, "Nor you, Schultz."

"We want all of you," the leader said.

No one spoke until Wilson broke the silence.

"But you said—," he started.

"I said we don't need what you used to be. We need Americans."

"Oh," someone said.

"What you said about the Scots, Mr. Wilson, I take to mean the Scots that fight for the Tories, because I'm what they call Scotch-Irish."

"Me too," several men said.

"Schultz there came from German people, and I guess that some of you had French or Spanish people in your line. If we are to win against the redcoats, we have to be as one."

The sergeant went back to the head of the line, and we moved on.

At dark, we stopped, and the men built fires. They mixed flour and water on pieces of bark and baked hard bread over the fires. Others cut green sticks and roasted pieces of meat. I helped get wood for the fires, and they shared their food with me.

After supper, the sergeant and two men came over to me.

"We have been talking," said the sergeant. "We want to know more about you. They say you come from Scotland."

"Yes."

"Most of the Scots who came here lately are for King George."

"Yes. I have met some of them."

"How do we know about you?"

"Oh. You think I may be a spy?"

"Some things you told us don't ring true. You said you were a bond servant, but bond servants don't wear good suits like yours—nor a coat like that."

The three men stared at me.

Chapter Thirteen

The Clans at Cross Creek

How could I prove to these men that I was for them? I told them how I got here.

"They made me a slave for five years," I said. "All I did was wear a tartan and sing a song they didn't like. Then there was Crouch."

I told them how I had met Crouch and later, McGill. They listened, but did they believe me? Then I thought of a way that I might win them over.

"I could be a spy for you," I said.

"How?"

"I will go to Cross Creek and find out all I can about the Tories; then I will meet you anywhere you say."

"Or tell them about us?"

"What can I tell them? That I saw thirty men somewhere? How would that help them?"

"You could join them."

"Never," I said. "The Scots who are for King George had to sign a loyalty oath when they came here. I have signed no such oath—far from it. Prince Charlie is my father's king and mine."

"We don't know much about Prince Charlie."

"Then maybe you know of John Witherspoon. He is a Scot who is for liberty."

"That's right. I heard him speak in Hillsboro last year," said one of the men.

"In fact," I said, "I have a plan for you."

"A plan? Are you a military man?"

"No, but I have read about the greatest general who ever lived, Alexander the Great."

"Ancient history," the sergeant said.

"He could win here just as easily as when he lived. What is more, he was a wise man."

"So?"

"He never fought unless he had to."

"Well, when the Tories march, we'll have to fight."

"If they march—but what if I can stop them?"

"You? How?"

"Sing them a song of Prince Charlie. Shame them out of fighting for the Hanovers. It would at least make them think twice about what they are doing."

The sergeant looked at the others.

"I reckon it would do no harm," said one of them.

"And I can spy for you while I'm there," I said.

"If they let you get away," said the sergeant.

He knelt down and drew a map in the dirt, marking out the rivers and creeks. He showed me how to get to Cross Creek; then he looked at me again.

"You have an honest look," he said. "I'm going to trust you with something. Find Dan Boyd. He can help you. For your sake, you better hope nothing happens to Boyd."

I left for Cross Creek the next day. When I was ready to go, I said farewell to Hugh Gordon.

"Good luck," I said. "I hope you don't have to fight the Tories."

"Yes, that scares me. Some of us may die. I guess I'm a coward."

"A coward? It takes a brave man to say that."

"I'm afraid to die," he said, "but I was more afraid of what people would say if I stayed at home. I've thought about it a lot, but this is the first time that I've talked about it."

"Maybe talking about it will help."

"I don't know. Should I make war or peace with the Tories?"

"I hope you make peace with yourself first," I said.

The sergeant gave me some hard bread to carry with me. I went alone but before noon, I came upon a small man with a backpack. He was Isaac Mendel, a Jewish peddler. He carried things in his pack to sell to farmers and their wives—things like buttons, buckles, needles, and even jewelry. He sold his wares in Virginia and around the eastern part of North Carolina. He came from Philadelphia.

"So where are you from?" he asked.

"Scotland. I'm a Scot."

"A Schottische Tory?"

"Oh no. A man named Crouch turned me against Tories."

"Clemson Crouch? A big Tory, that one."

We shook hands.

"I'm running away from a Tory master," I said.

"So don't tell the whole world. How will you live?"

"By my hands. I can grow plants, cut trees, or make things."

"What things?"

"Tables, chairs, and anything made of wood."

"Things people need."

"I hope so."

"It is true. I see no woodworkers in this colony."

"But I have to go where I won't be found."

"So change your name. Grow a beard. Join the Whigs."

We came in sight of a house. Isaac told me to go ahead and wait in some trees while he went to the door. He was at the house for a half hour.

"Any luck?" I asked when he came out.

"Yes and no."

"Can you live on yes and no?"

"You can't sell everybody. No sale here today. But luck. I get news."

"What will you do with it?"

"Take it to Cross Creek."

"To Dan Boyd?"

"What do you know of Dan Boyd?" Isaac frowned at me.

"He is the man I want to find in Cross Creek."

"Who gave you that name?"

"Some soldiers."

"So we will go to Dan Boyd's."

When we got there, we were hungry. The Boyd family gave us a dinner of pork and fresh cornbread. Almost a feast for me. I told Boyd my plan.

"The clans are gathering now," Boyd said. "Allan MacDonald is the key man. He owns a place west of here."

"That name sounds like someone I should know," I said.

"I hope so. He came to town last week and is calling out all the Scots he can get for King George."

"No Scot should fight for a Hanover," I said. "I'll try to talk him out of it."

"If you can stop him, you will stop the whole Tory army. He is staying at the Colin Campbell farm."

"Always the Campbells."

I went to the Campbell place the next day. It was a rich farm for Carolina, with a large house and a stable. Some horses were tied to a fence at the side of the yard. I went to the door and knocked. Someone let me in. I looked around the large room and saw several men at a table, playing cards.

"I have a message for Allan MacDonald," I said.

"Who from?" someone asked.

"I will tell him when I see him," I said.

"Oh you will? What's your name?"

"John Freeman," I said.

One of the men went to a closed door and knocked on it. "Someone here to see Allan Mac," he called.

The door opened and a man stepped out. He was older than I had expected, about fifty to sixty years old. Ever since Dan Boyd had mentioned his name, I was sure that I knew an Allan MacDonald in Scotland; but this man was a total stranger. My hopes of swaying him fell a little.

"Who be ye?" he asked.

"John Freeman," I said, "from Fife."

"A loyal Scot?"

"Aye," I said.

"I'll see ye later."

I could hear voices from the room behind him, so I took a chair near the door. Part of the talk in there was in Gaelic. I heard "Wilmington" and "Earl of Dartmouth." A man at the card table looked at me, so I sagged in the chair as if I were asleep. I made out more names from the talk in the other room. One was another MacDonald, a general. He and a colonel named McLeod did most of the talking. They were planning a march on Wilmington, and they would join some redcoats there. The leader of the redcoats had a name I'd never heard before, Cornwallis.

That was the last I heard. A woman came into the room and saw me. She came to my chair.

"Can we help you?" she asked.

I jerked upright, as if I had been sleeping. The woman was rather small, with dark, sad eyes. There was a dignity about her that made me leap to my feet.

"Excuse me," I said, with a bow. "I was tired."

"Of course," she said.

"I came here to see someone named MacDonald," I said.

"My name is MacDonald," she said softly. "Flora MacDonald."

Flora MacDonald. The woman who saved Prince Charlie.

Chapter Fourteen

Flora

FLORA MACDONALD. I stared at her like a dolt.

"I came here with my husband Allan," she said.

So that was why I thought I knew Allan MacDonald. Long ago, I heard that Flora MacDonald had married a man named Allan MacDonald—a distant cousin, maybe.

"I painted a picture of you once," I said.

"Really? Not from life."

"Oh no. I was young then and used my imagination. So it's really you? You are the most admired woman who ever lived in Scotland—for saving Prince Charlie."

"That was long ago," she said.

"When did you leave Scotland?"

"In 1774. We've been here hardly more than year, and now there is this talk of war. It is so sad."

Allan had come out of the other room and was listening.

"Flora is helping me raise an army for the king," he said. "Without her help, I would fail."

"That's why I am here," I said, "to ask you to stop."

"How now?" said one of the men with a look of surprise.

"Yes," I said. "Surely you won't help the House of Hanover. The same people who killed our men after Culloden."

"That's over with," said Allan.

"We made our peace with King George long ago," Flora added.

I went to the table and took up the deck of cards. I

shuffled them until I found the nine of diamonds. I held it up.

"The curse of Scotland," I said.

It was the card that the Duke of Cumberland chose to write a message on. The message was "no quarter." It sent two thousand Scots to their deaths.

"But that's all in the past," Flora said. "When Prince Charlie came, we fought for him. We wanted him for our king. We would never have fought to do away with the kingdom. Is that what you want here, no king?"

"No king and no redcoats," I said. "How can a Scot fight on the side of the redcoats?"

"Many a young Scot has had to choose between wearing a red coat and starvation," said a man at the table. "That's why I took one. Maybe the rich can afford to remember Culloden."

"I am not rich," I told him. "When I left Scotland, people still sang 'Will Ye No Come Back.' Have you quit that now?"

"We sing it," said Flora. "Aye, we sing it yet, but it is no war cry for us anymore. We say King George before raw mobs."

"Yes, many here are raw," I admitted. "Even such people as they deserve justice. How can they be loyal to a king so far away who refuses to hear them? Why must we honor liars and thieves just because they were born with a name?"

"But you can't win. England has power," Flora said.

"Who knows the future? Maybe France will side with us. Or Russia. Maybe Charlie will come back. What would you do then?" I asked.

Flora shook her head sadly.

"It comes down to the fact that we took an oath to be loyal," said one of the men.

"Yes, it's on our honor," said another.

"Some of us would lose pay or land in Scotland," said the first one.

"Some of us have kin back there, and we fear for them."

This was the same kind of talk that I'd heard in the

church at Winona. With Aunt Alice, alone now, back in Scotland, I was glad that no one knew my real name. I kept talking to them, but it was of no use. I was about to leave when a man came in and pointed at me.

"Arrest that man."

I looked at the man. It was McGill.

"He is a runaway bond servant," McGill said.

"Wait," Flora said. "Are you sure? He acts like a gentleman."

"Ask him."

"It is true," I said. "I tried to help a man. He might have been hanged for something he didn't do."

"You should have left that to the court," McGill said.

"What would you do if we let you go?" Flora asked.

I looked into her sad eyes. Of all the people in the world, I could not lie to this woman.

"Help the rebels," I said.

"A traitor," one man said.

"But an honest man," Flora said. "Be fair to him."

"We will," said an officer. Then he called two men from the table. "Lock him up. McGill can have him after we drive the Whigs out of Cape Fear."

I was right about their plans. They took me to the stable. We went into a room with a heavy door. The door was held shut by a hasp on the outside. I could see where a hole had been closed—a hole that would have enabled me to reach the hasp. One of the men saw me looking at it and grinned.

"Don't fret ye," he said, hitting the wood with his fist. "This door is a good one."

I saw a hole in the wall and a feed box near the door. The man pointed to it.

"A cook's helper will pass food and water to you through there."

"Rest ye," said another. They laughed, then they were gone.

I walked around the large room. The floor was covered with dry corn stalks and shucks. I pawed at them and found dirt below. If I only had a tool, even a wooden stick, I might be able to dig out. I searched every part of the room, but I found nothing.

At dark, I lay down. As I grew sleepy, I felt an itch. It started on my neck, next on my arms and legs, and then over my whole body. The litter was full of fleas.

I sat up. I couldn't sleep. Thoughts ran through my head about what would happen next. If the Tories won, they would surely take me to Hillsboro to be tried. On what charge? Treason?

I heard a rustle in the dry corn. It was rats. I clapped my hands and the sound moved away. There was silence for a moment, then the rats were back. How could I sleep? First the itch, then the rats, and, after midnight, the cold. As time passed, the cold became worse. I made a pile of corn litter and dug under it. That helped a bit. I got up and made a bigger pile, then I lay down and pulled it over me. At last, I slept.

Chapter Fifteen

Locked Up

AT MORNING'S LIGHT, I heard someone come into the stable. I looked through a crack in the logs and saw a young woman. She wore the coarse, undyed linen dress of a servant and a shawl over her head.

"Gruel," she said, as she put a bowl of steaming food into the feed box.

I saw a large iron spoon in the bowl. A digging tool. I grabbed it and dropped it into the litter.

"I need a spoon," I said.

"I brought one."

"See," I said, and I pushed the bowl to where she could see it.

"Maybe it dropped out." She stirred the stalks on her side of the wall. She opened a large door to let in some light. She stirred the litter again.

"I will get another," she said, and she left.

I picked up the spoon and stuck it in the logs of the wall where I could find it in the dark. The maid came back.

"Eat," she said, putting another spoon in the bowl. "It will get cold."

I dug into the bowl of boiled oats. As I ate, I watched the young woman. She turned her face toward the light, and I saw that it was an honest face. As if she felt my look, she turned back.

"What did you do to be a prisoner?" she asked.

"I'm alive."

"That's no crime."

"It is for some people."

"I think you must have done something."

"I ran away."

"Oh."

"Do you ever think of doing that?" I asked.

"No."

"Do you like being a servant?"

"I have to be. Always knew I would be."

"I did not plan to be one when I was in Scotland," I said.

"Are ye Scottish then?"

"Aye," I said, using the Scottish word.

"Then ye should like this gruel."

"I've had worse." I pushed the empty bowl back to her. "Thanks. It was really very good."

"That's my opeenion," she said and went out.

Late in the morning, she came back. She put something in the feed box and ran out. I went to the box and found a wedge of hot cornbread. It was filled with honey and tasted like cake. As I ate it, I wondered if I could get her to help me. No. That would make trouble for her.

I got out the iron spoon to see if it would work as a digging tool. The soil was loose and easy to move, but the going would be slow. I put the spoon away. It would make sense to sleep by day, when it was not so cold, and dig by night when no one was around. I crawled into the pile of litter and I dozed off to sleep.

Later, I heard the maid come in again. She put a bowl of stew and some oat cakes in the box.

"How long have you been here," I asked.

"A year. My father came to Carolina with the Campbells. He was to work for them, but he died at sea. I have to work to pay for our passage."

"That isn't right."

"Not right? I never think about that. It's the way it is."

"Does your master have children?"

"Yes."

"Will they have to work like you?"

"No. They will be ladies and gentlemen."

"No matter if they are good or bad people?"

"Yes."

"As it was in Scotland, but this is a new country. It can be different. How do you feel about King George?"

"He is the king."

"Who chose him to be king?"

"Are you a traitor?"

"Some call me that."

"I don't think you can win against the redcoats."

"We will see."

"If you did, who would rule?"

"We will elect someone."

"They say that many people here are ignorant. How can such people choose wisely?"

"They will learn. Who says that we are ignorant?"

"The Campbells. And others. They say you have no chance against the British."

"They don't know us."

"Are your ideas worth a war?"

"Do you think King George will give us liberty just because we ask him for it?"

"No. What is your name?"

"John Scott."

"A fitting name for a Scot."

"When I ran away, I chose a more fitting name, John Freeman."

"Do you live and breathe freedom?"

"Every minute. A taste of it is all you need to want it forever."

"I don't know," she said, looking out the open door. "What would you do if you were free?"

"I would get my head rights and maybe start a farm."

"Where?"

"Maybe here. Maybe in the Watauga land. They say that it's so wild there that no one heeds British rule."

"Is it good to have no law and no order?"

"That will come. If I stayed in this part of Carolina, I could work as a clerk—or I might go to college in New Jersey. I haven't decided just what I will do."

"I don't have to think about things like that. Just work."

"Because of your birth," I said. "In Scotland, we judged people by who they were too. It would be better to judge them by what they do."

"I don't know."

"Did your father ever own his home in Scotland?"

"No. He never talked about that. It was no use."

"If you have no property, you have no freedom," I said, quoting Rob Graham.

A voice called from the house.

"I have to go," she said, grabbing the bowl.

At dark, I bared a place in the floor near the back wall and dug at the earth with the spoon. I hid the loose dirt by clearing another area and spreading it out. Then, near morning, I covered the fresh soil with litter. I made a bridge over the hole with stalks and put loose shucks on that. At daybreak, the maid was back with gruel.

"How do you feel about King George today?" I asked.

"He is still king."

"In England. It's a long way to London."

"But they have ships and armies."

"I've heard that they hire Germans to fight for them. Do you think a hired soldier will fight as hard as a man who fights for his liberty?"

"The redcoats are regulars. You are beginners."

"But we are not children."

"No," she said, looking through a crack in the logs at me. I looked back.

"I have to go," she said.

After she left, I tried to sleep. I had too much to think about, but, at last, I slept. The maid woke me with my supper.

"I can't stay long," she said.

As I ate, I asked her, "Whatever happens with the Tories and the Whigs, can you and I be friends?"

She nodded.

"They will take me away from here."

She nodded again, then she smiled. "Will ye no come back again?"

"Do you know that song?" I asked.

"Aye."

"It reminds me of home. Sing it for me."

She began and I listened, my lips forming the dear old words, until she got to the chorus.

> *Will ye no come back again?*
> *Will ye no come back again?*
> *Bonnie Charlie, we can win,*
> *Will ye no come back again?*

She sang the rest of the song, but I hardly heard it. That line, "Bonnie Charlie, we can win," was the line I once made up and added to the song. I had heard it sung by only one other person: Jennie Duncan.

Chapter Sixteen

Free Again

I STOOD BY THE BOX, silent, until Jennie took the bowl. The Duncans had left Gour. I had thought they would always be there. Uncle Mark was master of Gour now. Duncan was a good man. He did as he was told when Uncle Mark gave orders, but his silence told how he felt.

Jennie was in my life again. Flora MacDonald was there too. So many Scots were there. There must have been a path in the sea from Scotland to Cape Fear.

There were such changes. Flora MacDonald was there too. So many Scots were there. There must have been a path in the sea from Scotland to Cape Fear.

The digging went slowly that night. The hole caved in, and the loose dirt was hard to hide. Near morning, I reached some grass roots outside the wall. I quit for the day. I was tired and eager for the gruel that Jennie brought for me.

"Tory oats," she said.

"Liberty oats now," I said.

"If you get another Tory master, how will you say then?"

"He won't be master of what I think, and someday, I'll be free."

"I could be too. Even now, if I choose."

"Run away?"

"No. Clemson Crouch, the magistrate, will buy my bond if I will marry him."

"No, Jennie, no. Don't do it."

"How did you know my name?"

"I...I heard someone say that Jennie would feed me. But don't marry Crouch! How long is your bond?"

"Four years more."

"How long with Crouch if he buys you and you marry him? For life, that's how long. What rights would you have?"

"What rights does any woman have?"

"Some have more than Crouch's wife would have. Be careful of whom you choose to marry."

"Choose? A maid has little choice."

"You can do better than Crouch. I know that man. He would make you a slave, and don't you forget it."

"Well, I haven't said yes, but I haven't said no."

"You're much too good for him."

"You hardly know me."

"I know you better than you think. I say that you can find a much better man than Crouch who would be glad to marry you."

"Name one."

"John Scott."

"Ye?"

"Why not?"

"Hoots. Are ye daft?"

"It's not so crazy."

"A prisoner? A rebel and a traitor? Ye will get yesel' killed before ye get yesel' married."

"A rebel? Yes. Join us."

"Will women do better with no king?"

"No worse, for sure."

"Belike a man will change his name when he marries, instead of the woman?"

"I don't know," I said.

"Did ye ever think of that?"

"No," I said. "But what's in a name? I've changed mine." More than once, I thought, but she doesn't know it. "I used to think that a name was everything," I said. "That was long ago. Now, I believe that what a person is and does means more than a name. I guess I wouldn't want to change my name after I am forty years old. Anyway, I expect we'll keep changing the names of women, not men. We can talk about it."

"Not now. I have to go."

I lay down and tried to sleep. Why did Jennie's speech suddenly turn more Scottish when I asked her to marry me? Had it shocked her that much? What did the future hold for me? For Jennie? Would she turn against me after I escaped? At last, these thoughts stopped racing in my head and I slept.

I awoke with a jerk. If the iron spoon was found here, Jennie would be punished. I quickly found it and rubbed the dirt off with a corn leaf. When Jennie came with my food, I pushed it into the feed box.

"Good," she said. "Mrs. Campbell has been asking about it. It looks good, not so rusty."

"I cleaned it with dirt. You should take all the iron spoons and rub them with dirt and sand. That will please Mrs. Campbell."

"I'll try it. Any other advice?"

"Don't talk to Crouch."

"I must, but I may not say what he wants."

"Good. And to me?"

"I say, can ye have no wee bit o' doubt on what ye are doing?"

"You can't be a doubter if you want to change things."

"Is change so good?"

"Good or bad, there will be change. We can only guide it. Jennie, I won't be a prisoner in a stable forever."

Oh John, it's not that. Our Lord was born in a stable."

"Is it just me?"

"It is your talk of war."

"Are you happy as a servant?"

"I try to be. When I was a child, I dreamed of marrying a rich man. Even then, I knew it couldna' be, so I gave it up."

"You see? That's what a king does. Tom Jefferson says we can have a country where virtue counts more than name. In such a land, you could marry any rich man you—"

"I didn't mean because he was rich. It was because I liked him."

"Oh, you mean someone you knew—"

Then I knew that she was talking about me. Should I tell her? No. Jennie and the rest of the world, must accept me as John Scott. What I would get as John Scott, I would earn. It was better than trading on a name. As John Scott, I was the same man I would be as James Gour. Or was I? Why had she liked me before?

"What kind of lad was he?" I asked.

"Spoiled. Green. He painted bad pictures that he thought were good, but I think he would have grown out of that."

"Then there is hope for me."

"Ye? Who knows? I have to go now."

"Good night, Jennie. Don't forget."

"Don't fret. Ye'll get gruel in the morn."

"I mean after I'm gone from here," I said. "Don't forget me."

She nodded and left. As darkness came, I began to dig with my hands. I reached dead grass and pried out bits of sod until I felt fresh air. I put my head through. There was no sight of anyone. I clawed at the dirt until I could get out. Past the corner of the stable, I saw the shape of the house. It was dark. I found the road and began to run.

Chapter Seventeen

A Message to Caswell

A<small>T</small> D<small>AN</small> B<small>OYD'S</small> H<small>OUSE</small>, I threw some gravel on a window. He let me in. Isaac Mendel was there.

"Isaac got here from Wilmington today," Boyd said. "We knew that the Tories marched on Sunday, but we didn't know where they were headed. Isaac says that they went down the west bank of the Cape Fear River. What do you know about it?"

I told him what I had heard at the Campbell place. Boyd nodded.

"So they want to join with the redcoats. We should get word to Colonel Moore."

"I can go," I said.

"Can you ride a horse?" he asked.

"Yes."

"Good. We'll get one for you."

We went to a nearby farm, and Boyd spoke to a man who had a pony. He gave me money for food and lodging.

"You can go faster than the Tories with their wagons. Try to find out how many men they have. Isaac says that Colonel Moore is somewhere on this side of Wilmington. Find him and warn him that the Tories are coming."

He made a map on a scrap of paper.

"Get some sleep before you start."

I slept at the farm until daylight. On the road, I went slowly. I stopped at Campbell Town to get news. Some said

113

that the Tories had more than a thousand men—maybe two thousand. Many of the men were poor Scots who had been promised land for service. I rode on.

Late in the day, I heard drums and saw men coming toward me. Tories. I saw a man point at me. There was a small church in a clearing with some horses and wagons around it. I rode in and tied my horse to a tree. The Tories were near when I went in. The room had the chill of the long winter in it, too much for the red belly of the little stove to repair. The crowd was small. A short, fat man was talking.

"And so he came here today, asking to speak. We welcome you, sir."

The fat man sat down and another man got up. He took a Book of Common Prayer to the front, then turned to face us.

"I am Clemson Crouch," he said.

I put one hand to my face to hide from him. I could hear men marching outside. Crouch read a prayer, then he spoke.

"I have come to remind you that we are part of the Church of England," Crouch was saying. "Beware of traitors."

As he talked, I kept my head down. I hoped that the short growth of beard on my face was enough to mislead him. When he was done, and asked for a song, the sound of the men outside had ended.

As the people sang, I noticed Crouch staring at me. I moved sideways in the pew to the end; then I walked to the door and ran to my horse. Which way would be safest? In the Tory army. I saw campfires behind me, to the north, and rode back toward them. A sentry stopped me.

"Who is it?" he asked.

"A Scot," I said.

"Password?"

"Drums for duty," I said. I had heard it at the Campbell farm.

"All right," he said, "but we changed it. It's 'Broadswords for King George' now."

I nodded. He was surely a lowly soldier—a private. If I could puff him up some way, he might want to show how much he knew.

"Glad to see you are alert," I said. "I've been looking for you all day. I thought you would be farther south, toward Wilmington."

"We got as far as Rockfish Creek. The Whigs were dug in there. We are going back to cross the Cape Fear at Campbell Town, and then cross the South River."

"I have no gun," I said. "If I join you, who do I see to get one?"

"I don't know. We don't have enough. The English took so many guns away from Scots after Culloden."

I thought, it serves them right.

"Will you get land for fighting?" I asked.

"Two hundred acres. And no taxes for twenty years. I came from Scotland five years ago and worked out my bond, but I had to sell my head rights. When England puts down this revolt, I will be a landowner."

I looked at him. His worn clothing was stained with the signs of hard work. I didn't want to annoy him anymore.

"I'll join the others," I said, and led my horse toward a campfire. I stopped before I got to the fire and waited until the men had rolled into their blankets. Then I took the horse into the trees and headed back south, around the sentry. The church was dark when I passed by it. At Rockfish Creek, a Whig stopped me.

"Friend or foe?"

"Foe of the king," I said.

I asked for Colonel Moore and gave him the news that I got from the Tory sentry.

"Good work," he said. "They must be planning to cross Black River at Corbett's Ferry. We need to tell Caswell."

"Can I do it?" I asked.

"Yes. He should be at Corbett's Ferry now. Go south on the east bank for about ten miles, then west to the Black River to get to Corbett's Ferry."

He took my map and added some lines to it.

"Tell Colonel Caswell to hold the Tories at Corbett's Ferry if he can. If he can't, we'll stop them at Moore's Creek. After you talk to Caswell, ride down to Moore's Creek and tell Lillington to dig trenches on the east bank. Get some sleep now. You'll need it."

I rolled into a blanket by a dying campfire. At dawn, I was on the road again. I found Caswell two days later near Black River. Soon after I got there, we heard drums on the west side of the river. Tories. From time to time, we heard shots. I left Caswell and rode to Moore's Creek.

At Moore's Creek, I ate and camped with the men and helped them dig a trench on the east bank. On Monday, the 26th day of February, Caswell and his men arrived from the north.

"The Tories got around us," a man told me. "They crossed Black River a few miles above the ferry while some of them made noise to keep us there."

"This bridge is where we'll stop them," Caswell said. "Take off the floor and grease the beams. Some of you stay out here on the west bank with me, in case they show up first."

Men began prying off boards while others put tallow on the rails. By dark, the job was done. Some of us built fires on the west bank, near the old road, to make the Tories think that our main camp was there.

"Now let them come," Caswell said.

A short time later, some men came out of the trees carrying a flaming pine knot and a white flag of truce.

"Don't shoot," one said. "We want to talk."

"Come on then," Caswell said.

"Give up your arms," said a Tory.

"If you will take an oath to support the king, we'll pardon you," said another. He was one of the men that I had seen at the Campbell place. I stepped back into the shadows. One of the Tories was looking right and left, trying to size up our camp.

"This is your last chance," the Tory leader said. "If you don't give up now, you will be tried for treason. That means death."

"Or victory," Caswell said. "Our answer is no."

I listened to the Scots as they spoke about loyalty to the Crown. As James Gour, son of an earl, I felt that Scots should not be for King George. As John Scott, bond servant, I wanted liberty. It felt good to be helping the Whigs.

"We say forever, no," Caswell said.

"Then we shall meet again,"the other said, and the Scots left.

Soon after they were gone, we moved to the east bank of the creek. Even though we knew about the slick beams, it was hard going. We crept across, one man at a time. We each used a long pole as a cane to stay on the rail. Below us, lay the still water of Moore's Creek. It looked like black glass until we pushed the pole into it, feeling for the squishy bottom.

When we got to the east bank, a new group of soldiers had joined us. Hugh Gordon was with them. As the night passed, I sat in a trench and talked with him. The winter cold seeped into us like lamp oil into a wick. A fog formed over the creek and settled in pools around us. We wrapped our blankets tightly around us and stopped talking. Hugh looked at me, and I knew that he must be thinking about the same thing I was—the one thing that we hadn't talked about. We were thinking about what would happen the next day.

Chapter Eighteen

Moore's Creek

As the darkness turned to gray, I heard someone speak. I looked around and saw some of our men moving about in the fog; then they were gone and it was suddenly lighter. I must have dozed again for a few minutes.

I shook myself awake and looked at the men around us. One gave us a sign to be ready. What was I doing here? I wasn't a member of any army. I had no gun. Should I go? I knew it was too late. If I ran, it might start a panic. I sat back down and waited.

Then we heard it. Out of the mist came a wail that sent chills down our spines. The sound grew louder as another wail joined the first one, and louder still as more wild voices howled at us. Men peered into the fog, straining as they tried to place the sound. I looked at Hugh. His hands shook on his gun.

"Wh-Wh-What's that?" he asked.

"Bagpipes," I said.

We heard the drums next. The sound of their beat came out of the fog. Gray ghosts began to move toward us, then they were men. They came kilted and armed; some with guns, some with swords alone. They were Scots. The sight of them and the scream of the pipes gave me chills. They were my people. I rose to my feet, thinking that I should be with them. I remembered then that they marched for King George, and I dropped back into the trench.

They came to the bridge, driven by the wailing pipes and throbbing drums. Some Whigs, who had gone out at the first sound, ran back to the trench on our side of the creek. One of the Scots called out in Gaelic. They had seen that the camp on the far bank was empty. One man stepped out of line to fire at the running men on our side. Then they came on.

When they reached the bridge, they stopped for a moment when the front men saw the stripped beams. Then they started across. The first two men stepped out onto the slick rails. I saw the look of surprise on the face of one as he fell. He grabbed at the beam and missed, landing in the water. The column of men clumped behind the bridge.

"Use your swords," a man shouted as he started across. He punched at the rail under his feet with the point of his sword to keep his balance. He was Colonel McLeod, one of the officers I had seen with Allan MacDonald. He reached our bank and waved his sword.

"Forward," he called.

Several Scots reached our bank. They fanned out and came at us. I felt naked without even a sword to defend myself. A man near me called out, and the men in the trenches fired. McLeod fell, and the volley cleared the bridge. Men were flopping around in the water; some were wounded and others were knocked off by their falling comrades. McLeod crawled toward us, then got to his feet. He waved his sword.

"On," he called.

He came at us again, following the point of his weapon. Behind him on the bridge, men swayed about, trying to keep from falling. More of them were on our bank now, behind McLeod. The Whig guns roared again. The fire cut down the Scots who had made the bank. I heard the mixed sounds of horses screaming, men groaning, and more guns firing. I saw men twisting in pain and death.

On the far side of the creek, someone yelled orders, but his words were lost in the din. Men ran to and fro. I looked

at the bridge again and saw a man in the creek near our bank. It was McGill. He slipped under the dark water. I leaped up and ran toward him.

"Down," called a voice behind me as the firing went on.

I made it to the bridge and dove, meeting McGill as he came up. I pulled him to a tree root on the bank, and held to the root with one hand and to him with the other. When he was able to hold to the root, I pushed him out of the slippery slime and onto the bank.

"Are you hurt?" I asked.

"My leg," he said. Then he recognized me. "'How did ye get here?"

His right leg was broken. I looked out and saw that the battle was over. The Scots on the far bank had broken and run. Some Whigs were fording the creek to chase them. I called for help. Two men came over and we made a carrier for McGill from some poles and a blanket.

"You could have been shot," one soldier said.

"He would have drowned," I told him.

We took McGill to a house not far away, and the soldiers went back to pick up prisoners. I followed them. A captain asked me to help write reports on the prisoners. Most of them were poor Scots who had come to the colonies recently. The officers were men of property. A private told us that old General MacDonald, who had been at Cross Creek with Allan and Flora MacDonald, became ill the day before. The younger, more reckless Colonel McLeod took over.

"He was daft," the man said.

"Aye," said another.

We took all of the Tory weapons, and I asked for a sword. I passed by several heavy broadswords and found a lighter one—the kind my fencing master had used. As I strapped it on, I heard a prisoner give his name.

"Tom Cane," he said. It was the man who had lied about me to Captain Chase. As he looked at us, I saw that he didn't know me. Two and a half years in Carolina and a half-grown beard had changed James Gour into John Scott.

I found Hugh Gordon and asked if he would help me. I told him what to say, then we went back to the prisoners.

"Tom Cane," Hugh called out, pointing at him. "You are wanted for the murder of James Gour, son of the earl of Gour."

"No," cried Cane. That's not true. I never killed him. No one killed him. He was shipped over here."

"There is no record of James Gour in the colonies," I said.

"That no means he is dead," said Cane. "They called him John Scott. I signed a paper to that. Sam Lynch paid me to do it."

"Then you are guilty," I said.

"They would have taken me in place of him. It was me or him, they said. The old laird's brother was behind it."

Uncle Mark. Why had I never suspected him?

"Will you sign to that?" I asked.

"Aye. But I never killed anybody."

I asked Colonel Caswell for some witnesses. He sent a captain with Hugh, Cane, and me to a justice of the peace. When the papers were done, they took Cane back, and I went to Wilmington. I found the magistrate who had met with us when we got off the ship. I showed him the paper that Cane had signed.

"I want my bond cleared," I said.

He read the paper.

"Pay the clerk to file these," he said.

It took most of the money that Boyd had given me. Luckily, I had been eating with the army and sleeping on the ground. I paid the clerk and saw my name go down as James Gour.

"Will you go to Scotland?" the clerk asked.

"Maybe," I said.

"You will have to join the Tories for that."

When I left the clerk, I realized that I must choose between two lives. I could either go on as John Scott, a rebel, or as James Gour, an earl. As James Gour, I must get passage on a British ship to claim my land in Scotland. As the clerk had said, I would have to become a Tory to do that. What should I do?

I found an inn and stayed the night, wondering what I would do next. When I went to sleep, I dreamed of Scotland. I was on the road again, then near the old castle—my castle. There was Jennie, waving some flowers, then I awoke. Why this same old dream?

I thought about the last few years of my life, mainly the ones spent in Carolina. The hard work at Smith's had been enough for a lifetime. As James Gour, there would be no more of that. As James Gour, it would be sweet to take revenge on the people who had misused me.

What about Jennie? How would she fit in? Could she be Lady Gour? No, that would never do. I could not take a housemaid back to Scotland as my wife. Yet she was always in my dream. Maybe it was because the last time I saw the old castle, she was there. That was it. I had been homesick. I wondered if Elizabeth MacTay was still unmarried.

I stayed in Wilmington until the money that Dan Boyd had given me was gone. Then I remembered the farmer who owned the horse I was riding; he would want it back. I left the coast and rode to Cross Creek. As I rode, I made some plans. First, I must go to the Campbell place and tell Jennie my real name. That would end any plans she might have of marrying me. Then I would return the horse. After that, I would go to Scotland.

When I got to the Campbell place, Jennie was hanging some clothes on a fence to dry in the sun. I stopped. She looked at me as if she saw a stranger.

"It's me. The one they called John Scott," I said.

"I know who you are," she said in a cold voice.

"What's wrong?"

"You helped them kill Mr. Campbell."

She ran into the house, I might have followed her, but I didn't want to face the family then. Anyway, I was free from my promise to Jennie.

I took the horse to its owner. Along the way, I suddenly began to feel very tired. I needed to find some place for a long rest. But where? I thought of Rob Graham. He had wanted me to visit his farm. I told the farmer, and he knew of a family going that way in a wagon. The farmer's wife gave me some food for the trip.

On the first day out, the sky was clear except for a few stringy clouds. Riding in a wagon was easy, but I felt more tired than ever. The next day was warmer, but the sky was gray. I felt sick. The wagon driver told me to lie in the back of the wagon and rest. My face felt hot, and my body hurt with each bump of the road. Each day was darker than the day before until snow began to fall. Then I left the wagon and took to the woods on foot. The north wind came at me, and I felt as if the fog from Moore's Creek had gotten into my bones.

I found Winona and the church. Rob had pointed out the way from there, along the creek.

"Look for a big tulip poplar," he had said.

Late in the day, almost frozen, I saw a huge tree ahead. I heard a dog bark. Then someone called, a woman's voice. I saw a young Indian lass come toward me. Was this an Indian village? Then I remembered that Rob had told me that he was going to marry a Cherokee woman named Sarah.

She met me as I fell. I heard her call out and felt someone carry me. I was put on a bed of straw and given a hot drink. A tea made from a brew of birch twigs, spice bush, and sassafras—Indian medicine. I drank the steaming cup and lost track of time.

Chapter Nineteen

Fever

OUT OF NOWHERE, bagpipes wailed and drums pounded like cannons. Where were they? I looked at the dirt floor around my bed and saw little men in kilts marching. When they fell down, men in red coats took their places. Another line of men—dressed in rags—marched against the redcoats. Time after time, the men marched, but I never saw the finish. I wanted to know how it would end, but I was always left in suspense.

The war would go away when strong hands held me up and other hands put soup or tea to my mouth. Gentle hands wiped my face with a damp cloth. God's grace was in the hands that tended my feverish body.

After many lost mornings, there was a morning that I knew as morning. With the weight of fever still on me, I tried to get up and I fell.

"Too weak," someone said, and drew a blanket over me.

More days and nights passed. I heard voices. Then, one day, a new but familiar voice. I saw Isaac Mendel take off his pack and look at me.

"What news?" Rob asked.

"Clinton came to Cape Fear from Boston with an army of redcoats. He heard about Moore's Creek and sailed away."

"The Scots?" I asked.

"Prisoners. Eight hundred. Some go free if they promise not to fight again."

"How many killed?"

"About fifty. But what happened at Moore's Creek will save lives. If the Tories won, the colonies would split."

"Will we have independence?" Rob asked.

"There is talk of that now." Isaac turned to me. "Did McGill find you?"

"McGill? No."

"He got a pardon. He put up posters offering money for anyone who finds you."

"McGill has no claim on me now. I have papers," I said.

"No more talk. You are weak, so eat. Here," Isaac picked up a plate of food that Sarah had set before him, "Have a piece of bread."

I took the hard cornbread and chewed on it. Isaac talked to Rob for a while, then he left.

After that, I gained strength with each new day. I began to go out of the cabin; then I helped Rob cut trees and dig sprouts. After a week of that, he said that it was time for me to go.

"Ye can get some land and start a farm," he said.

"There will be time for that later," I told him. I would tell no one yet of my plan to go to Scotland.

"It will soon be planting season," he said.

"I owe you too much. I can never pay you and Sarah for all you've done, but I can at least help you until summer."

"Ye owe us nothing. But do as you please," Rob said.

"I'll stay."

I stayed until late July when Isaac Mendel stopped again.

"Cornwallis came to the cape from England, but when he heard about Moore's Creek, he sailed on south," Isaac said. "Moore's Creek upset their plans. There's a meeting in Philadelphia now. All of the colonies sent delegates. North Carolina started it."

"Started what?" I asked.

"A call for independence. That was back in April. Moore's Creek helped that too. People who were on the fence now say that we don't need a king."

"Good. What other news?"

"McGill sold his farm. Six families will go to New Scotland—or Nova Scotia. They are all at the Campbell place near Cross Creek. He still has the offer out for you."

I laughed.

"So laugh. You can hide here. I won't tell him."

"Hide?" I said. "I don't have to hide. I have papers."

"Maybe you should show your papers."

"Yes," I said, "and I'll be rid of it. I'll go to Cross Creek."

I went alone, wearing the sword I got at Moore's Creek. I would show McGill the papers and be free of his claims. What if he tried to have me arrested? I didn't want to fight anyone, but I was glad that I had learned swordplay from a French master.

Chapter Twenty

Back to McGill

As ISAAC HAD SAID, McGill was at the Campbell farm. When I got to the yard gate, I saw him sitting on a log stool in the shade of a tree. He saw me and got up. I dropped one hand to the hilt of my sword and swung the gate open with the other.

"Where ha' ye ben, laddie?" he asked, coming with his hand out. "I have something for ye."

I shook hands, watching him all the while. He took me to the porch and rapped on a post there. Jennie came out. She smiled.

"I heard about the saving of Mr. McGill," she said.

"Bring us John's papers," McGill said.

Jennie went in and came back with a leather packet.

"The bond is in here," McGill said.

Jennie watched me study the papers. McGill had signed them, giving me my freedom.

"We are going to Nova Scotia," she said.

"So I heard."

Another young woman, wearing a fine dress, came out.

"We thank you for saving our friend," she said.

"Yes. We are glad that Mr. Campbell has been found. We pray that he will be pardoned soon to go with us," said Jennie, resting her hand on the arm of the other woman. The woman looked down at Jennie's hand. Jennie, who was smiling at me, didn't see the look.

"They need you in the kitchen," the woman said sharply.

Jennie snatched her hand away and went inside. McGill went with me to the gate.

"I owe ye more than these scraps of paper," he said. "I wouldna' be here but for ye. What else can I do for ye?"

I looked around and saw that we were alone.

"There is one thing, but if it is done, it must be done in secret," I said.

"Say it, and if I can do it, amen."

"Jennie's freedom."

"Jennie? The maid?"

"Yes. You could tell the Campbells they have to give her up to get Mr. Campbell pardoned. I know some Whig leaders; I can speak for him. Tell Jennie that it will cost too much to take her with the Campbell family, but tell no one that I asked it of you."

"Aye. I think we can do that." He looked at me and smiled. "So it's Jennie ye—"

"It's not that," I said. "I knew her long ago. As a child. She doesn't know, and I don't want her to know. I'll never see her again."

"As ye say," he said, shaking his head.

I left the Campbell place with two sets of papers. One set proved that I was a free bond servant, John Scott. The other set proved that I was James Gour, the ninth earl of Gour. In Scotland, it would be good to know that, as John Scott, I had earned my freedom. I went into Cross Creek with high hopes for the life that lay ahead of me. I wished that Jennie had been born a MacTay, but Elizabeth would be right for me was the wife of an earl. I was thinking about the MacTay land when I heard a voice call out.

"Stop. Stop that man."

I looked up into the window of a brick building where a man pointed a finger at me. It was Crouch. Another man came out, an officer of the court, and faced me. He looked back to Crouch.

"What is the charge?" he asked.

"He is an escaped bond servant. Ask to see his pass."

"Well?" the man said to me.

"I don't have to show a pass to any man," I said, loud enough for Crouch to hear.

The man dropped his hand to his sword. I could tell by his movement that he was no fencer. I could best him in a sword fight, but I knew that he was only doing his duty. Crouch was my enemy, so I went inside.

Crouch went to a table and sat down. I put down my papers from McGill. Crouch looked at them.

"McGill is a fool," he said; then, all at once, he grabbed the papers to himself and said, "Take his weapon."

I leaped onto the table and drew my sword.

"Wait," I said to the officer. "I don't want to hurt you. My French fencing master taught me how to use this when I was a lad."

"French fencing master," Crouch said with a sneer. But the other man didn't move.

"Read this," I told Crouch and took out the paper signed by Cane. "But if you think to take these, they are filed at Wilmington."

I set the point of my sword on the paper, pinning it to the table. As Crouch read the sheet, the color left his face.

"Earl of Gour?" he read, almost in a whisper.

"Yes," I said. "I am the ninth earl."

I picked up the paper with the point of the sword and flipped it into the air and caught it with my left hand.

"A good blade," I said, patting it. "In the past you have said some bad things about me, Mr. Crouch. You called me a traitor. You said that I lie. Those words don't go with me. I believe, among the gentlemen you favor, those are reasons for a man to ask for—"

"I beg you...I had no idea," he began, his face now the color of dirty snow. He stared nervously at the sword in my hand.

"Are you quite sure that I am a free man?" I asked.

"Oh yes, of course. I only believed what others told me. I am sorry."

"What about the papers that you took?"

With a shaking hand, he laid the packet from McGill on the table near my foot. I stepped off the table to the floor and took it. The other man watched us, a trace of a smile on his face.

"We are done now, Mr. Crouch," I said, and walked out.

As I walked along the street, I felt sure that Crouch would never again annoy me. I had often thought of taking revenge on him. I no longer cared about that. "Vengeance is mine." Rob was right. It would do me no good now to look for revenge. I felt a new kind of freedom that I had never felt before.

I saw some people gathered around a man at a square. I stopped to see what he was saying.

"They've signed a paper in Philadelphia," he said.

"What kind of paper?" I asked.

"A paper that Tom Jefferson wrote—a declaration—a Declaration of Independence."

"Huzza," someone shouted.

"Was John Witherspoon there?" I asked.

"Witherspoon? From New Jersey? Yes, he was."

People were running across the street to tell others. Up and down the street went the word. Independence. What would it be like to live in a country where all was new—even the laws? Would there be justice? Not always. I had seen enough of life now to know that. There would always be men like Crouch and that woman on the porch at Campbell's. How she looked down when Jennie put a friendly hand on her arm. She looked down with scorn because Jennie, in a happy moment, forgot that she was not the equal of someone else. I thought about the feeling I got when I saw the woman's look.

As I went along, I realized that it would be like that in Scotland. I would be the one who looked down on other people. Did I want that?

I stopped. A man came by waving a piece of paper.

"Independence," he yelled.

I turned and went back the way I had come. All at once, I saw the two lives I could lead in a clear light. I didn't want to be in the same class as Crouch or the Campbell woman. I would stand with Tom Jefferson. I would stay in America.

When I came in sight of the Campbell place, I saw Jennie. She was at the side of the yard, near a fence, gathering flowers.

"Jennie," I yelled.

She looked up and saw me; then she raised her hand with the flowers high, waving to me. I began to run.